MC [illegible] ES

AND OTHER STORIES

CATHERINE
FINCH

Chaffinch Books

For my family –

who have played an essential part in
creating so many happy memories that
continue to spark my imagination.

Introduction

Story collections invite the reader to browse, to skip to an engaging title, to pick up the book and put it down at will. A novel has time on its side; time to reveal the characters, the plot, the themes. Short stories burst onto the page, each word heavy with significance, sometimes leaving the reader to expand the narrative long after they have finished reading.

The stories in this collection capture a moment in time. Some are based on personal experience, others on the lives and loves of characters from my novels. The rest, I have to admit, are a mystery in their origin. Just as people you have never met appear in dreams, so characters emerge from the imagination and find their place in a story.

Books are a precious gift to readers. We line our shelves with them, collect unread novels to pile at our bedsides and occasionally lend to friends, our name neatly written in the front cover.

If this book has found its way to you, when you have read it please add your name at the back, then set the book free by passing it on to a fellow reader with the reward of witnessing their joy at receiving a gift.

And insist that when they have finished reading, they give it away.

Catherine Finch

January 2021

Contents

It's a long way to Penzance

September winds use the station as a tunnel. They blow from southern lands bringing grit and strange smells and a restlessness which stirs the waiting passengers, flapping at coats, scarves, hair. There's a thread of summer, a draught of spice and a hint of promise from a distant climate that will stay soft, even in winter. Indian summer – well, the winter will be harsher, nothing's for free up here in the north.

The station is a place to pass through, when the journey's direction changes or begins or ends, and disgorged travellers rejoin the real world, some noisy and animated, others quietly seeking the anonymity of the crowd.

A father holds his daughter's hand, looks along the line, worry grooving his face. Relief lightens hers. This is the month of departures; to university and college, a journey to a new life, an escape from the old. The train arrives, a platform clears, fills, then empties. New travellers collect and stand in patient expectation, glancing at the illuminated board, ears straining to catch the flat-vowelled announcements.

Further along the freezing platform, a woman stands alone. Emma looks for a bench – a place where she can be quite separate, no greeting, no friendly smile to give or to take from a stranger. There it is. She heaves the rucksack from her shoulders to set it upright on the floor. A man walks by with a cup of brown liquid in a plastic beaker, steaming, spilling in droplets on the concrete floor. He slackens his pace. Emma looks at the cup and is taken back to the hour spent in Preston Police station the previous day and once again she feels as if she has been torn apart then hastily, wrongly reassembled in a rush to clean up and tidy away.

'I want to speak with someone about my husband,' she had said to the woman on reception, rehearsed confidence underpinning the sentence, then with less certainty, 'about him hurting me.' There, it was done, the words finally spoken aloud. It was done.

'You want to report an incident?'

'Yes, yes, I suppose I do.'

She was taken to a room that smelt of cleaning fluid, sweat and something sweet that Emma couldn't identify. Two male officers, one straining hotly in his uniform, the other plain-clothed, sat opposite her. Plain Clothes stubbed out a half-smoked cigarette. Mugs of black coffee sat on the desk, the surface scarred with rings.

'I'll get you one if you want,' Uniform said, '5p from the vending machine.'

She refused. They took her details. Then Uniform said, 'You're reporting a domestic violence incident against yourself by your husband. Is that correct?'

'Yes.'

He stared at her face as if searching for bruises, cuts, grazes. He found none.

'Tell us about the incident.'

'He just hits me,' she whispered.

Plain Clothes wrote this down.

'Once? Is this an isolated incident?'

'No.'

'Many times?'

'Yes.'

'How long has he been hitting you?'

'Since we were first married, three years ago.'

Uniform shifted in his seat. Plain Clothes tapped his pen on the table.

'And you've never made a complaint before?'

'No.'

'How does he hit you? Where?'

'He,' she faltered. 'He slaps me.'

'Slaps you.' Plain Clothes wrote again. 'Does he ever punch you, kick you?'

'No.'

'Where does he slap you?'

She hesitated, shame burning her cheeks. She whispered, 'Where it doesn't show.' The words hung awkwardly like a lie.

Uniform looked at Plain Clothes without expression, but she saw the invisible thought pass between them.

He said, 'And you don't want him to hit you?'

Emma slammed both fists on the table with a thump that made the officers jump.

'Of course I don't want him to hit me. Do you think I'd be sitting here telling all of this to you two … men, if I wanted him to hit me?'

The air in the room seemed to thicken. They shifted uneasily in their plastic chairs.

'I think,' said Plain Clothes, 'I'll see if a WPC is available.'

The police woman brought a chair round to Emma's side of the desk.

Emma had to repeat everything. It sounded silly, childish, petulant. No, he doesn't punch me, no he's never slapped me in the face, no I have no marks to show you and yes, he can be very loving.

'When did you marry?'.

'May 1974, over three years ago.'

The woman sighed. 'I'll make you some tea, do you drink tea?'

Emma nodded. While the WPC was away, she put her head in her hands, tears dripping onto her skirt. If she could remember the way out she'd leave now.

The WPC backed into the room with a tray. Emma looked up as she placed it on a side table. It was a perfect setting of teapot, milk jug and two cups and saucers.

'I can't drink policeman's tea,' she said. 'Brought these in from home so I could do it properly.'

She poured the tea and passed it to Emma who sipped, grateful for something to occupy her hands, to distract her senses.

'Tell me more about your relationship. Take your time.'

Emma took a deep breath.

'He wants to take away my whole life, myself, the person I am. He wants to control every little part of me as if I am a small child. He says he loves me, but I don't love him. I don't think I ever did. I've tried to leave, but he says marriage is a promise forever, for all time. He once said we would both be better off dead than divorced.'

The policewoman listened to Emma's description of her marriage, passed tissues, wrote nothing down. At last, she spoke.

'I have to tell you that this is unlikely to come to court,' she said. 'Emma, you don't have to stay with him. I can give you addresses of safe hostels, or maybe you have a friend you could go to?'

Emma said nothing. It had been a mistake. No one here could help her. She reached for her bag and stood up.

'Yes,' she affirmed, hearing a surprising note of confidence in her voice. 'You're right, I should leave him.' She went for the door, desperate to escape, then she turned and said, 'You know, leaving him will be easy.' She looked straight at the other woman, 'but he will find me.'

The station clock chimes two. She glances around, notices a black UK passport on the floor by her bench but one is rushing to claim it. She takes it and opens the passport. A serious young man stares back at her. She finds his name, age, place of birth. A train ticket to Penzance has been tucked in the front with a sheet of paper, folded in half. She opens the sheet and reads.

Pete, thanks for travelling with me on this part of my journey. We have lived, we have loved and now we must part.

Carol x

A shadow darkens the page. Emma fearfully raises her eyes. It is the face in the passport looking back at her.

'Oh,' she says, relief flooding her body. Realising her invasion of something so personal she stammers, 'I am so sorry.' She refolds the letter, hands everything to him.

'That's ok,' he says. 'I'm glad you found them.'

He sits on the bench beside her leaning forwards to balance a rucksack, even larger than her own, strapped to his back. He offers a hand.

'I'm Peter.'

She shakes his hand.

'You're cold,' he exclaims.

'It's normal. Sorry.'

'Don't be.'

Emma thinks the serious face in the passport is, in the flesh, rather sad.

He skims the letter.

'I'm sorry,' she says again.

The man smiles. 'You'll have to stop apologising for things that aren't your fault. It's over with Carol, time to move on. Nothing lasts forever, does it?' He screws the letter up, tosses it neatly into the nearest bin.

'I'm going south,' he says, 'to Cornwall, to live in a commune.'

'I'm going north,' Emma replies, 'to Carlisle, to stay with a cousin who doesn't really want me.'

'Why?'

'I suppose,' Emma admits, looking at the stranger, bewildered at her sudden desire to explain everything to him, 'I suppose I'm running away.'

'From?'

'From my life as it is now, as it was. From all of it.'

He ruffles his hair, turns to look at her. She sees concern in his gaze. A tear escapes when she blinks. She brushes her cheek roughly.

He touches her arm. 'Don't run to someone who doesn't want you. What sort of an escape is that?'

'It's a terrible one,' she admits, 'but I've nowhere else to go.'

'Come with me. Come to Cornwall.'

Emma stares at him and her whole life rolls before her, white like a canvas, ready for brush strokes in sweeps of colour, her colours, the ones she has mixed and is brave enough to use. 'You're still young,' the policewoman had said. 'Make a new start, go away from here,' but the thought of it had filled her with dread.

The track hums, people stand, gather belongings, walk forward. Her ears swell with sound.

Suddenly, the Penzance train is upon them, filling the station with metal and glass and a great heave of screeching brakes, but above the noise, the whistles and the blast of warm air, Emma shouts, 'Do you know, I think I will.'

He stands and stretches his hand towards her. The serious, sad look is broken in a sideways smile.

'I've no ticket,' she says.

He shakes his head, shrugs.

'Take a risk, get one on the train, hide in the loo.'

'I've never ...'

He reaches for the carry strap on her bag. She puts a hand in his and lets him pull her from the bench.

A surge of delight whips through her body, emerging in a giggle, then a laugh, fuelled by the thought of freedom, complete and wild. She tosses her head, walks towards the train, her eyes on the door where passengers are waiting. She glances right.

A tall figure, eyes panning the scene, seems to catch her eye. It's a man in a suit clasping a green travel bag. She knows the bag, knows the man. He is striding, then he starts to run, and she hears her name cutting a swathe through the noise of the platform.

Peter turns, taking in Emma's face and the man.

'My husband,' she says. 'He wants me.'

'And you want him?'

'No.' The word punches the air, vehement, bitter.

He pulls her towards the train door. She hears her name again, closer this time. Fear hastens her feet and she tightens her grip on his hand as they fall into the train. Peter stows the bags, takes the window seat and puts an arm around her. He glances towards the platform.

'He's looking in all the windows, keep your head down, rest on my shoulder as if you're sleeping.'

Emma pushes her face into his neck and breaths in

the woody smell of his Parka. She feels her pulse like a beat.

'He's standing back now, there's nothing he can do. He's walking away, he's gone.'

Doors slam, the train shifts, a jolt, a pull, then a gathering of speed.

She looks up.

'Where am I going?' she asks.

He takes her hand.

'Wherever you want. It's your life, not his.'

Emma wishes she could believe him, then starts to rehearse her tale of a lost ticket.

As the train finds a smooth, even speed, Peter removes his coat, nods at the guy opposite, turns towards her. She feels his breath on her cheek.

'Tell me everything,' he says.

'It's a long story.'

He grins. 'It's a long way to Penzance.'

I spent many hours on Preston station when I was a student at Charlotte Mason College in Ambleside. In the late seventies and early eighties, it had a great little kiosk stuffed with chocolate bars, which invariably tempted me to a purchase.

It was always draughty.

Losing the Luck

Ernest

Rain, a leaden sky, thunder clouds that press the life out of you. I touch the varnished gate, darkened by the wet. Five coats it took. I did that for them. Came here every evening, sometimes at night. Ignored her at home; I'd lost interest. When Tom left us to marry his sweetheart, we both lost interest.

They were young, excited. It's a little house, stone, not Accrington brick and there's a carved lintel above the blue front door – pretentious colour, but she insisted. He carried her over that threshold. Bloody hell I envied him. He swept her up as if she was a child and the look she gave him told me I wasn't wanted. He waved at me before shutting the door, and I noticed the horseshoe door knocker drop. It was hanging wrong, losing the luck.

I've come because it's still loose. Another slam and it'll be off. I know she's not in; I can't face her yet, but I can do this. I open the gate and walk up the path. It's an easy job, but I struggle to get the screwdriver in the head of the screw. My hand trembles and it's a black anger, not cold or nerves or old age. I give up and stab the paintwork, once, again, then over and over, sometimes scratching, jabbing until the door is pitted and scarred. The screwdriver falls to the step.

I bellow my grief at the cold stone before I leave.

Maisie

The sun is out by the time I turn up the street. He is there, slamming the gate, an arc of droplets catching the light. He's striding, running to get away. I call out, but my legs ache and my insides are threatening to heave again. At the gate, I steady myself and look at our house. It gives me a good feeling, and I know the leaded lights in the bay window will be scattering jewels across the parlour floor.

I look up and see a loose slate, out of place in the neat, glistening rows. A week it had taken us, me passing them up the ladder, Tom dancing across the roof like a cat. He wanted everything right before he went off with the Pals, as if he knew.

Then I see the front door. It's damaged, vandalised, the knocker still hanging awry. I pick up a screwdriver. Has Ernie done this? But there isn't time to wonder. I open the door, leave the key, and bolt to the scullery sink where I heave up my dinner.

I drink from the tap, and touch the glow in my belly. At the door, I find the screw, take the screwdriver, and right the knocker, fastening it firmly to the wood. I give it a gentle rap and take a step back to see the sun catching the wet surfaces.

'I love you,' I whisper.

The evening light in my eyes, I set off to find Ernie.

The Accrington Pals was a battalion raised in the early months of the First World War in response to Kitchener's call for a volunteer army. Groups of friends from all walks of life in

Accrington enlisted together. In its first major action, the battalion suffered devastating losses in the attack on Serre on 1st July 1916, the opening day of the Battle of the Somme. This proved particularly harsh to a community where nearly everyone had a relative or friend who had been killed or wounded.

This Flash Fiction piece was awarded third place in Flash 500's quarterly competition in May 2015.

Slaters Bridge

I was never close to my mother. She was a loud-mouthed woman with a hearty laugh, a rasping, vicious tongue and a liking for gin. What she earned at the Salutation Hotel, she spent at the bar and she never seemed inclined to make a home for us. The front step was slippery with moss. Weeds grew from the slate walls. If we had wood or coal, Mam lit the fire. If not, we froze. We ate left-overs from the hotel kitchens but I don't remember her cooking a meal, or cleaning, or making the beds. I went to school in dirty clothes until I was old enough to wash my own.

I enjoyed learning, but at fourteen, she made me leave school and found me a job, cleaning. She scorned my liking for books, stopped me visiting the Quaker meeting rooms on Sundays, talked incessantly about how I must attract a man.

So I did, only it wasn't the man she meant.

When Mam found out, the unholy row roused every nosy old crow on Peggy Hill, and a gaggle of shawl-wrapped figures gathered by our cottage. I'd never seen her so mad, first at me, with blows of a flat hand to my face, then at him, and this time her fists found his head, his chest, his belly, until he shouted she must stop.

'You bastard,' she repeated, spitting the words into my step-father's face. 'She's fifteen, a girl. You dirty bastard.'

He took his coat from the peg and left, his glance in my direction told of regret and shame.

In the morning, as I retched in the privy, she stood by the door and said I would have to go to Aunt Mary's farm in Langdale. Mr Birkett, who had a car, might take us for a favour. I hadn't seen my Aunt Mary for years, although Mam said she cared for me when I was a baby. The sickness invaded my body with a misery so complete, I couldn't have cared less. Mam said she'd better come with me, but couldn't get a night off work, so would walk back the same day.

She put my few clothes in a bundle, tied it in a great knot and looked at me, her face creased with anger.

'You're ruined,' she said. 'You know that? Who's going to want you now? You should've told him to stop, pushed him off.'

I hung my head, put a hand on my stomach and contemplated the floor. To speak would invite further retribution. To remain silent had much the same effect, but demanded less effort on my part, so I kept my lips together.

We waited four days for Mr Birkett to take us. In the end, Mam came back from his house in a fury, said he was a miserly old faggot and she'd let his tyres down. The next morning, we got up at sunrise and walked. She marched, I trudged, my shoes too large, my socks full of holes so the bare skin rubbed and chafed against the leather. A relentless drizzle soaked our clothes, making the cloth heavy and cold, and when low cloud drifted in to cover the fells there was no point looking anywhere but at the path beneath my feet. Seven miles to Little Langdale. We had a quick break at Skelwith to drink a scoop of water from the river Brathay and shelter under a tree, then we laboured on, our own thoughts for company as we barely exchanged a word the whole way. Eventually, we turned along a mud-covered lane to a cottage and farmyard.

Mam knocked on the door, once, then louder. A voice called, the sneck clattered and a figure stood there.

'Edward,' she said. 'I'm here with Anna.'

'Come in,' he replied, his voice low, the accent strong. 'We'd heard.'

I'd never seen a house so neat and clean. Boots lined up under coats and hats, and the table was scrubbed to a whiteness I wanted to touch. The range glowed, its heat filling the room with comfort and there were no cinders or ash to dust this tidy hearth. My glance was taken to a shelf of books, but I was too far away to read the spines.

A woman came in, a small boy holding her hand. She was wiry, strong-looking, with a brown face and dark hair tied up in a scarf. This, I knew, was my late father's sister. She nodded at me, looked at Mam, offered no greeting, but her expression was open and I sensed kindness. The knot in my chest began to ease.

'I knew you'd come,' she said, her expression giving nothing away. 'You should've left the lass with us when Robert passed – we offered.'

'I couldn't part with her, then,' Mam said. 'She was all I had.'

'She was all *I* had.'

'I see you've been blessed.' Mam indicated the boy.

'Yes, four years ago. If you leave her, she'll not be coming back this time, do you understand?'

Mam glanced at me, her face a mask of hardness, her mouth sneering.

'Appleton's son was interested, wanted to court her. She's a pretty girl, could've found a good husband to take care of her, and me. But they're all laughing at her now. She'd be lucky to get the half-wit who hangs around the market cross.'

She handed over the bundle, told me to be a good girl, which seemed a strange thing to say in the circumstances, and left. I stood in the kitchen, the walk back home in the rain seemed more desirable than staying amongst strangers.

Aunt Mary came to me with a softer look and bid me sit at the table.

'You hungry?'

I shook my head. 'Sick,' I said. 'Nothing stays down.'

'How about a dish of tea, then?'

I nodded, and as she prepared it, placing bread and cheese on the table, I lay my head on my arms and sobbed.

The family sat and ate as I sniffled. They talked about ordinary things, teased the boy, passed plates and made a game of forking pickles from the jar as if I wasn't there. A chair scraped and I felt a small hand on my knee.

'He wants to know who you are,' Aunt Mary said.

I sat up, wiped my face with a damp sleeve and tried to control my breaths. I smiled at the boy, reached for the tea and sipped. It tasted rich with creamy milk, far better than the weak brew Mam served up, the tea used many times before she threw the leaves in the yard.

Aunt Mary touched my hair.

'We'll have to do something about that,' she said.

'What?'

'Crawlers. We don't have them in this house.'

My Aunt bid Uncle Ted take the child away for an hour and she dragged out a tin bath, filled it with hot water from the range and sat me in it with a bar of soap and a soft-bristled brush. As I worked at the dirt on my skin, she soaped my hair, then poured pans of warm water over my head, the sensation bringing on delicious shivers. By mid-afternoon, I'd been scrubbed as clean as the table. I sat on a stool in borrowed garments that hung over my thin frame, pulled in with a belt, as my own clothes soaked in the bathwater. Aunt brewed more tea and tempted me with a morsel of bread and jam. I took it and nibbled cautiously, the sweetness seeing off some of the nausea.

'That baby won't grow if you don't eat,' she said, the chiding edged with kindness.

'I don't want it to grow.'

She took a breath, towelled my hair vigorously, then she finger-raked the tangles before starting properly with a fine comb. I protested when the tugging became unbearable and before long she stopped. I heard a sound, a snip, then another and matted shanks of blond hair fell on the stone flags. I didn't protest. I knew I was infested and to be rid of the creatures would be a relief, but I cried as my hair fell to the floor and she shushed me in soothing tones. When she had finished, she wrapped a scarf around my head and tied it under my hairline at the back of my neck. She reached for her shawl.

'Come on,' she said. 'We'll check on the boys, then I want to take you somewhere.'

The mist was lifting. The sun, a pale disc behind clouds, shone weakly over the fells, gaining strength as grey sky gave way to wider patches of blue. I followed my aunt down the lane. We climbed over a style, continued for a short way along the path, then descended to the beck. I was treading carefully, watching my feet and the back of her head. Suddenly, I looked up and saw the prettiest bridge I had ever set eyes on. It spanned the water in an arch of slate from the far bank to a huge boulder in the middle of the stream. A slab of stone completed the crossing.

'Slaters Bridge,' Mary said.

I repeated the name.

'It's been here for centuries. Built for the pack horses to travel to and from the coast.'

She took my hand.

'Let's cross.'

The steps were uneven and slippery with rain, but the wide stone was smooth and level, easy to walk across. As I put a foot on the arch, sunlight flooded the valley and brought the beck to life with sparkles on the water. We stood together and looked over the handrail, our shadows dark on the green-grey river bed.

For the first time in weeks I felt a glimmer of hope.

'I come here when I need to think,' she said. 'And you must come, too.' I felt a hand on my arm. I opened my mouth to say something, but a strangled, unfamiliar sound came out.

'Thank you,' I managed to whisper, then added, 'why are you kind to me?'

'You're not used to kindness?'

'My step-dad was alright, until ...' I faltered, shame making me blush.

Aunt Mary didn't speak for a moment and when I looked at her, her face was contorted in disgust. Surely, now, she would send me back.

'It was my fault,' I stammered. 'I led him on and he didn't understand when I said to stop.'

'He told you that?'

I hesitated, thought about Step-Father's words after he'd finished with me. 'Yes, I suppose he did.'

'Well it's not right,' she snapped. She took both of my hands and gripped them, pulling me around. 'It wasn't your fault, Anna, and he should have stopped.'

'Can I still stay here?' I asked in panic. 'I can't go home.'

'You're my brother's daughter,' she said, 'and I loved him. You were precious to your daddy for a short while. Of course you can stay here.'

There was sadness in her face, but I couldn't share it as I'd never known my real father, and as Mam didn't mention him, I had no image to make him a real person. At once, a thought led me to hope he was like his sister.

'When you were a child,' Mary said, releasing my hands, 'I brought you to stay with us when your Mam was so full of grief she couldn't look after herself, never mind you. I wanted you to stay. I couldn't seem to bear a child to full term, so I was desperate to keep you.'

I watched a twig bob on the current, then catch itself in a swirl of glistening water, caught for a moment, then rushed downstream on the swollen spring torrent.

'Did you lose some babies?' I dared to ask.

'Yes. Most in the first months. I kept one a bit longer. Then, after ten years of nothing, I knew I was expecting again, and I also knew that this one was here to stay. You must want your baby, Anna. It didn't choose to be conceived. It deserves a chance.'

The sky had cleared, now, and I felt glad Mam wasn't walking back in the rain. I looked around, listened as the breeze rustled the leaves. The scent of earth and grass and water was familiar, comforting.

'I've been here, before,' I said.

'You remember?'

'No, but I can feel it.'

'You came here many times with me. As a baby, you were a crier, that's for sure, but I could always soothe you if I brought you here. You used to go quiet, as if you were listening to something.'

For a while we stood on the bridge, the beck swirling beneath us. I held the slates with both hands and was filled with a sense of deep calm. The sun on my back, I closed my eyes and listened to the voices of long ago, men and women crossing this footbridge, each leaving a trace of their lives.

The sickness diminished to a whisper in my gut, a reminder of the life I was carrying, and I knew that whatever happened next, I had come home.

Slaters Bridge is a 17th Century packhorse bridge spanning the River Brathay. Historically, Little Langdale was at the intersection of packhorse routes leading across to Ravenglass and the Cumbrian coast, as well as Keswick and Penrith in the North Lakes, and Ulverston, Broughton-in-Furness and Barrow in Furness to the south.

The bridge is a beautiful place to pause, take in the beauty of the surrounding fells and reflect on the travellers who would have been grateful for its passage across the beck.

Ducks First

He shoved her to the ground, waved his shotgun at the ducks.

'Ducks first, then you,' he said, dropping beside her on the dew-soaked grass. He grasped her hand, touched his lips to her wrist.

She shuddered, pyjamas lying cold and damp against her legs. She wore nothing else under the coat he had flung at her as he ripped her from sleep and dragged her outside. Her bare feet found hiking boots by the door, but the tough leather scratched and chafed toes that wept blood for a cushion of socks.

The tears had dried up. Sobs rose in bubbles, bursting with great shudders, wrenching her shoulders.

He gripped her icy fingers, one hand on her, the other tight on the gun.

'You left me,' he repeated.

'No ...'

But pleading was useless. She knew that in his mind the order of things was set.

God knows she had tried to understand his need for neat lines, exactness, perfection. Sometimes he was pleased and smiled, then rage coloured the room red and he flung everything aside, including her.

When she explained she loved him but had to leave, she saw confusion in his face, incomprehension. But there was no violent reaction, no rage or anger. She thought she'd got away with it. She thought her friend's empty cottage would be safe.

Dawn broke with a grey and blue shiver, the early light emerging sadly beautiful, soft.

'Ducks first, then you, then me,' he whispered, as if his words were an expression of love.

He released her, positioned himself on one knee, aimed the gun at the drake. She felt the fear drain and her body fill with a cold, clear calm.

In the face of death, she thought. I am unprepared.

She stood up delicately and when he turned to her, she bent to kiss him on the forehead.

He looked back along the barrel of the gun.

'Careful,' she said, taking her fear and anger and desperation, releasing it as a bolt of energy through the toe of her boot, catching him roughly under the chin. The gun left his hands. She grabbed the barrels and swung it through a huge arc to slam the side of his head.

He reeled, shouted, his mouth a ring of hurt.

She fired.

The shot flung them apart; he blasted backwards, she knocked off her feet, unprepared for the stock ramming into her chest. She staggered upright, her finger on the trigger, ready for a second blast.

He roared in pain and anger, gripping his stomach as he gasped for air, then he hit the ground and rolled into a moaning, rocking ball, blood veining his hands.

'Duck's first,' he bellowed raggedly. 'Not me, not me.'

He tried to stand, but her next shot found a deadly mark.

The echo died. Silence held its breath. A splash disturbed the lake and a pair of mallards took flight over the torn ribbon of pink sky.

The characters in this rather sinister piece are imaginary although their narrative, which is about possession, control and an unhinged mind, reflects a theme frequently explored in fiction, often based on true stories.

Ducks First began with the title and the final image of birds flying away at sunrise. The actions linking the beginning and the end, told from the woman's point of view, are pure fiction.

Paid in Full

I found him in the river; leather boots, trouser legs, soldier's jacket. His face rippled under the quiet water, the features separating and reforming. Curiosity gripped and I stared.

I recall pushing him with my toe, watching the body move like the logs and branches that float downstream after heavy rain and catch between rocks. I glanced around, then slid two fingers into his pocket teasing out a whistle and a penknife and a photograph of a lady with dark hair. Finally, before panic, and the urge to escape overtook me, I released a few small coins.

A boy of strange and curious ways, I was a collector; pebbles, rusty shards of metal, coloured glass, animal bones. I risked friendship to steal ribbons or pencils from the other children. I risked punishment if my aunt found my treasures, so I hid them. A loose floorboard in the barn could be prised up, or a brick removed from a wall. Discovery haunted me; harsh fingers handling precious things, stealing my collections. In the end, a careless hiding place twisted the course of my life, destroyed the lives of others and loaded my soul with a bitter, impossible debt.

Today, my head is full of disturbing thoughts and the afternoon heat oppresses. I refuse my cane, but I am grateful for Fabienne's arm and the tall figure of my grandson close by. She is a sweet girl and I see the love she has for Stefan.

'Do you feel up to a short walk?' she asks. 'Surely you want to see the village now we're here. We can return to the car if you get too hot.'

She tells Stefan to fetch my hat, and it is placed gently on my head.

We walk and I notice the cart, abandoned long ago, as if the horse was released for the last time and the carrier let the shafts fall to the ground. As we pass, I pause to touch the letters of his name, faint colours across the rough planks. I remember myself as a child of three who sat in this cart and howled all the way from the station. I stopped when my uncle gave me an unexpected cuff and shouted; 'Shut up, that's enough.'

Should I go into the village? So much time has passed. Yet someone may recognise the turn of my head, a strand of hair, a look that unsettles a memory. I grip Fabienne's arm and we walk towards the *Maison de Maitre.* She remarks how pretty it is. Stefan fiddles with his expensive camera. He is a collector of photographs, a safe, two-dimensional pastime. Later, he will tinker with the images on a screen, enhancing colours, smoothing imperfections, polishing the captured memory.

We pose in front of the gates.

'Do you remember this house, Papi?' Fabienne asks, and I reply that I do. She sees the geraniums tumbling over the balustrade which frames the double staircase leading up to the door. Years ago, my aunt had grumbled at this extravagance.

'They need two staircases?' she protested to Uncle Jean. 'Madame doesn't have to sweep them herself, that's for sure.'

I look up to the flowers, the twisted ironwork, the crafted stone, but I see soldiers, Monsieur Delpech in pyjamas, his face red, his eyes full of fear. I see a woman crying, children clutching at her dress. The sound fills my ears. Fabienne's chatter, whilst not unpleasant, seems distant.

It is a cloudless sky and I am glad of my hat. I wear long trousers and sleeves now, after all, who wants to look at the thin arms and shapeless skin of an old person? Yet as a child, I put on the same rags every day; garments fashioned from curtains, old clothes, even the sacks that held the grain. My aunt was as resourceful as the rest during the occupation, but only when her own children had been clothed did she look to me.

The little bar tabac is still here, and I recall the dark interior, thick with cigarette smoke. If Madame Celeste had sweets, we huddled around the counter with our coins and were usually rewarded with a morsel of something pink or red which brought a brief shot of sugar to sweeten our lives. Our fathers and uncles sat with glasses of pastis, the alcohol softening their faces, gentling their hands. On the farm it was a cuff or a slap. In the bar they ruffled heads and patted shoulders. The figure of poor Jean-Marc is still clear, a noisy, ebullient drinker, dragged home by his wife most evenings. We would watch, then mimic his drunken capers, each of us exaggerating his loose limbs and slurred voice. If the soldiers came in, the men drank up and left, coins placed quietly on the counter.

The bar is closed, so we walk on towards the *Mairie* and the church.

'How pretty,' Fabienne exclaims. 'What beautiful stonework.'

I hear the click of the camera behind me. City youngsters. They see the charm of this village. I gaze at the steps leading to the church door and I see desperation, injustice, and I feel the burden of shame I shouldered as a boy and have carried for a lifetime.

We sit outside the *Mairie* and they leave me to rest as they visit the church. Stefan takes Fabienne's hand. She reaches up and kisses him with a smile full of promise. I am jealous of their youth yet grateful they can enjoy it. At their age, I was already old.

A crowd of us would meet at the river, but the day I saw him I was fishing alone. I wanted to run, but found no movement in my legs. The urge to search his wet pockets, to take possession of whatever I found, took hold. With dripping fingers, I stowed the items in my bag and briefly glanced at his face. It was pale, like the flesh of a dead fish, stripped of its silver scales. Turning away in disgust, I fell over a rock in the shallow water and splashed wildly for a moment, trying to regain my balance. Calm tipped into panic and I reached the bank with frantic, ungainly strides. The firmer ground gave my legs momentum and they sprinted me back to the village, my stolen goods rattling.

My mind was already working on a hiding place. It would be too dark to make things out in the barn, so I chose the wall opposite the post office. A loose stone came out easily. I stashed my treasures and hesitated before replacing the stone, choosing one coin to keep. Turning its foreignness over in my fingers, I walked home through the village, catching my breath.

'Where've you been?' My aunt was waiting. 'Disappearing again, when you have jobs to do. Get on with them before it's too dark.'

Dodging her raised hand, I touched the surface of the coin in my pocket and felt glad.

'Papi.' A voice weaves through the memories and I feel a gentle touch on my arm. I turn my head and see Stefan's face.

'You're tired,' he says. 'Shall we go back?'

I think about this.

'We can go past the post office,' I say. 'It isn't much further that way.'

Fabienne eases me to my feet and we make our way between the houses. The road is dusty, hot. Shutters are closed and there is no one to notice us. She tries to lead me to the pavement, but I resist and we continue across the road to the hiding place. It isn't there. I needn't search for it as the wall has been rebuilt. There is one stone, slightly larger than the others, with a metal plate, a little tarnished, but the lettering is clear. Fingering the small coin in the pocket of my trousers, I reach out and touch the finely etched names: *Arnaud Delpech, Celeste Balat, Jean-Marc Fournier. Mort pour la France.*

'Did you know these people?' Fabienne asks, and I nod, but offer no explanation.

'How sad,' she says, and the three of us stand in quiet thought. And I remember.

Soldiers marched in, tearing apart a soft grey dawn, shouting orders in harsh, twisted French, clattering on doors. We were herded towards the square, some still in night clothes, others rough-haired and unwashed. I was sent to get my cousin, who was at the pump, and on the way, I witnessed the mayor being dragged from his home.

Men held their wives, women grasped their children. In the faces around me I saw defiance, hatred, fear, and I twisted my fingers to stop them shaking. Officers stood on the steps to the church. A whistle, a penknife and a handful of coins lay on the floor; my treasures, discovered. I tried to speak, but we children were pushed to the back where the school teacher encircled us with his arms whispering words of calm. We heard accusing voices, then shouts, then cries.

Finally, three shots.

As the marching feet receded, a subdued wailing began, rising up until words of fury punctured the sorrow. Children found their parents, but I crept away and hid in the barn.

When my aunt and uncle returned, they dragged me from my hiding place. She pinched my arm and pressed her wet, angry face close to mine.

'What do you know?' she hissed. Madame Delacroix saw you hiding something in the wall. And what's this?' She held out the German coin. 'I found it in your pocket.'

My cheek took the full force of her outstretched hand as she shouted, 'Tell me.'

'The body, it was in the river, it was already dead.' I faltered over the words. 'I – I just took some things and hid them.'

The fury was uncontrollable, her hand, a fist, her mouth venomous and foul. In the end, my uncle dragged her away. The last words I remember were, 'My friends, they are murdered because of you.'

I touched the hurt places, watched tears drip through my fingers to the dust and felt each sob like a rough shock. Darkness fell and I was afraid to be alone. I wiped my nose and face on my sleeve and reached up to try the door. It was jammed from the other side. I pleaded, rattled the wood. Each time I stopped and listened, I heard only the stirring of the animals and the frantic clicking of the cicadas. My bare foot touched something under the straw. Reaching down, my fingers closed around the coin. I lay on the straw like an animal and slept.

The next day, Uncle took me to the station and put me on the train to Paris, back to my father.

I feel the softness of Fabienne's hand. She lifts the brim of my hat to look into my face.

'Why did you want to come back?' she asks. 'I think you have a story about this village that you haven't told us.'

I push my hat from my forehead, try to recall why I decided to return after so many years, and, in the muddle of my thoughts, there is one clear thread, and I know.

'I have a debt to repay,' I offer.

'From so long ago? You were only a boy.'

I am silent. My thinking, like my limbs, is slow. I need time to separate each thought and drop it into place.

'Papi, you are the kindest man. You have spent your life helping others.' She looks again into my face and I briefly lift my eyes to meet hers. 'Whatever happened when you lived here, you have paid your debt.'

I consider her words. I think about the three who paid for me. In my life I have tried to pay, so many times, in so many ways, but I have discovered that release from the magnitude of my wrong comes at an impossible price. The Bank of Atonement is, indeed, a foreboding place. No withdrawals at this establishment, only deposits against huge, life-sapping debt.

'We love you Papi,' Fabienne says, and I meet her eyes with a slow gratitude. She takes my hand between hers, but does not ask for more.

So many years ago. I was such a little scrap of life.

As we pass the cart on our way back to the car, I feel in my pocket and draw out the small German coin, worthless now, priceless as the means to finally settle my account. I have carried it for far too long. It is time to let go. I look briefly in the palm of my hand, then I push the coin into the soil beneath the flowers, burying it deep. I experience some lightness, perhaps it's the heat, but I know that a final reckoning has been settled.

I glance towards the young people striding out in front, hands touching. Their lives, their memories are untainted by war. Hope is in the next generation. It envelops me, opening my eyes to truth, offering a chance of peace, finally.

And my debt to this village, to Monsieur Delpech, Madame Celeste and Jean-Marc, paid in full.

Monteils is a village in the Aveyron in the south west of France. Every year, an old cart, tipped up on its shafts, is planted with a breath-taking display of summer flowers.

The bar, the manor house with two staircases and the square are a short distance away. A war memorial on the way to the river ensures that we never forget the lives lost during both world wars.

The story is fictional. The historical setting is not.

The Bath Short Story Award attracts over 1000 entries from around the world and in 2017, eighteen were selected to feature in the anthology of winners. Paid in Full was one of those stories.

Skinny Woman

He made the trip alone. Andy, his brother, had urged him to fly, but it was the long drive, the miles then kilometres, punishing and relentless, that gave Chris a purpose. Once in France, he had really put his foot down in an angry, and at times, dangerous manner. There was something reckless and uncaring and totally out of character in the way he drove and he felt ashamed. But he didn't care if he had an accident. He didn't care if he was caught by a speed trap. How could you care when everything in your life that was worth caring for had collapsed so suddenly and so finally?

He had to stop near Orleans and instantly regretted his choice of service station. Once through the fuel queue, he grabbed easy food and paid with his credit card, grunting a miserable, *Merci*, at the checkout. The darting French children, who seemed to form noisy groups then dash apart only to regroup, irritated him with their boisterous youth. They seemed untouched by the heat, which had him feeling damp and oppressed. His stomach growled, but was rewarded bleakly with apples and chocolate bars grabbed from the bag on the passenger seat, swilled down with gulps of warm soda. He arrived in the south furiously tired, but feeling that something had been achieved.

His brother Andy, and sister-in-law, Hannah asked nothing from him. They provided food and wine and work, and that, for Chris, was a start.

'Just do it automatically,' Hannah said. 'Put the food in your mouth and the drink to your lips. When I tell you to carry this or paint that, just do it, don't think about it. Don't try to get over things or see the future –

it's too early yet. You have to manage living, existing, keeping your body going. The mind will come later.'

So Chris did as he was told, and Hannah was right. By the end of four weeks, during which time he had started to eat again, had developed more than just a taste for the local wine, and had painted the longest fence around any foreign field, he had talked, shouted, cried, and scoured the sore places inside him until they felt clean and empty and sad.

He thought about his wife with a white-hot anger. She had shown little emotion when she left him, announcing that her affair with a colleague had made her realise she didn't love him anymore.

'We've had 26 great years, Chris,' she said. 'I think we both need a new start.'

It was alright for her. Her *new start* had been expected, planned secretly and with excitement, grown into her life for over a year. She looked happy, her face glowing.

He came to France expecting nothing. The gite business was hard work and Andy and Hannah were too busy to pander to his misery. But on some nights, when all the guests were happy and there were no sinks to unblock or pools to clean or stupid questions to answer, the three of them would sit late into the warm evening drinking and talking. Andy would give in to sleep first and stumble off to bed. Then Chris and Hannah, words gently slurring, eyes heavy, sometimes with hands touching, would mine the depths of his hurt until she supported him to his attic bedroom.

Once, while the rest of the family slept, he pulled Hannah onto his knee and put his arms around her spare frame. They were all thin in his brother's family.

Andy was strong but lean, the three children tough and bendy like bits of wire, with skinny legs in loose shorts. He put his hand on Hannah's thigh, then over the sharp bone of her hip, then he pushed under her vest top to spread his fingers out across her ribs.

'I love you,' he said drunkenly. 'I can feel all of you, all your muscle and bone, your heart beating. Diane was too fat, I could never touch her like I can touch you. I never got to the core of her.'

His hand crept higher, but Hannah stopped it.

'No,' she said. 'I know what you need and I can't help you, Chris, but if it wasn't so morally wrong, I could easily take you to bed.'

'And I could easily let you,' he said, regret in his voice, relief in his head.

He left at the end of the summer. It was a calmer, less frantic drive back. He arrived home in the middle of the night. Diane's car was on the drive, forcing him to park in the road. He was irritated. Why couldn't she leave her car at her lover's? But when he unlocked the door, he saw at once that the house was untidy; a bag in the hall, crockery in the sink. He could sense a presence. She was there.

If he's here, if they're in my bed, I'll throw the pair of them out, he thought, taking the stairs two at a time.

But she was alone in the clean sheets of his bed – the bed he had changed before he left. He said her name and she sat up.

'You're home,' she said.

'Why are you here?' he asked.

'We've parted. It was a mistake, Chris. I had to come back.'

She reached out to switch on the bedside lamp which illuminated her hair, her face, her round shoulders. She looked at him. 'We need to talk,' she said.

Chris shrugged. 'I need to sleep, it's been a long drive. I'll go in Matt's room tonight.'

'There's no need,' she said. 'You can ...'

'Oh, but I can't,' Chris interrupted. 'I can't.'

He left her, feeling no emotion, no anger, no relief, just an overwhelming weariness, as if the needs of his body had shut off his thoughts. He collapsed on the bed in his son's old room.

She was in the kitchen when he came down in the morning. She smiled at him but he couldn't return anything more civil than a nod and a good morning. She started to cry, to tell him how the affair had ended and finally how sorry she was. Chris felt nothing.

'It's too late,' he said. 'We can't get back together as if nothing happened. I'm ready to move on. You said we both needed a new start, well I've started.'

She came to him, sobbing, put her arms around him, began to plead with him. He held her gently finding her body thick and solid. Why had he never noticed that before? He recalled his sister-in-law's long limbs, her shoulder blades, sharp above her bikini top, the tiny wrists which he could easily encircle with his hand.

He wasn't a vindictive man. He didn't want to hurt anyone, but the words came from the very small place inside him that was callous and unfeeling, and revenge-seeking. It was carelessly, thoughtlessly delivered. There was no doubt that it would deeply wound his wife. He pushed her away.

'There's no going back,' he said. 'Can't you make it up with him, try again? It's over between us, Diane.

And anyway, next time I'm looking for a skinny woman.'

The novel, **Holding On Letting Go,** *began as this short story. Chris emerged so strongly as a character he almost demanded I take his narrative forward.*

Although the story didn't win any prizes, it was highly commended by the judges in a competition for authors who live in France.

The Olive Oil Man

She scowled as her mother dragged the trolley from under the stairs. It had once been a smart, sponge-down plastic shopper with a neat buckle fastener. It could have graced the streets of Paris, led purposefully by a chic Madame, who filled it with plump cheeses, fresh green beans and artichokes, a jaunty baguette too long to fit beneath the cover.

But this trolley was destined for a grey town in northern England; a town of soft rain, wet pavements and grit. It had run through puddles, been hauled onto the rear platform of double-decker buses, shoved into the luggage space under the stairs to fall on the ankles of a slouching conductor. Years of over-filling with bottles and tins, and vegetables that wept juice into the lining, had stained the red tartan, split the seams, bent the flimsy axle.

Dad had rescued it with masking tape and staples so now, the person dragging this monstrosity was not only guilty of a flagrant lack of style, they were also displaying the inability to buy new.

'I'd rather go to football with Dad,' she protested.

'No, you wouldn't,' Mum said, reaching for her coat.

'Or stay here on my own.'

'I need you to help, love. Let the boys go off to football.'

It was a token gesture of defiance, played out every week, feeble in the face of her mother's determination and the unwritten rule that on Saturday afternoons girls went shopping, boys went to the match.

Francesca had grown up with a strange sense of separateness, but as the only girl after three boys, it was hardly surprising. It wasn't uncomfortable, it gave her a sense of uniqueness in the family. Yet it came with a notion that there was more to unearth, and one day, if she was patient, she would understand.

But why did her parents choose such an exotic, unusual name for her after John, Michael and David? She loved her name, loved the sound of the soft *c* and the *s* and then a hard *c* before the final *ah*. It stood out in the register after Jill Garth and before Susan Jones. Francesca Elizabeth Hunter; an author's name, a singer, someone special, someone to be discovered.

She didn't resemble the rest of her family, although Granny once said she had her mother's high cheekbones. In fun, Grandad called her a little cuckoo – but only once. She remembered laughing, making cuckoo noises, then realising there was tension between the adults and no one else was laughing, not even Grandad.

Tall and strong, with rough blond hair and blue eyes, her parents and brothers were impatient, loud-voiced, confident. The boys played football, Dad refereed, Mum stood on the side with flasks of tea and sandwiches pulled out of the shopping trolley. Francesca was slight with narrow bones and a thin face. She was dark-haired, hazel-eyed and hated sport.

When Mum ranted at the side of the pitch, she lost herself in a book; as her brothers trained, she drew in her notebook; as they all watched the local team on television, making enough noise to have the neighbours banging on the wall, she sat upstairs and wrote stories.

But she always, always felt loved.

Her brothers teased her gently, looked after her

and protected her. Dad never shouted at his daughter, as he often did at the boys. He read to her when she was small, took her to the cinema, checked homework and encouraged her to work hard at school and she loved him unreservedly, claiming his attention in the quiet, patient way she did everything.

Her parents both worked, but money was tight. Every Saturday afternoon, Mum took Francesca to the market on the bus. They took the old shopping trolley as it was the only way to cart everything home.

Blackburn had an indoor market hall, high-ceilinged, cold in winter, stuffy in summer. Francesca was in awe of the stallholders with their red faces and hands, who added up in their heads and shouted across to each other in a loud and confident way. They were masters of their world and they knew it. Her mother was at home in this place of noise and sharp humour, playing one trader off against another to get prices reduced.

When Francesca was little, she was handed morsels of cheese from the cheese man, an apple from the fruit man, a boiled sweet from the sweet lady. Cold, rough hands touched her cheek. When she grew older and learned how to set her face in an expression of boredom, the fussing stopped and her task was to pull the trolley. She would keep her hood up or hang her hair over her face.

Yet in a quieter row, behind a wall of fabric bolts and curtaining, the sounds of trade were absorbed in the dusty air and the smell of old vegetables and fish was replaced by garlic and herbs and spiced vinegar. The Italian stall, its high counter heaped with pastas in cellophane packets, always fascinated Francesca. No boiled ham or tripe or piles of pink flabby sausages here. Jars of green and black olives lined the shelves and strings of dried salami the colour of blood hung from silver rails. Olive oil was displayed in litre bottles, green and mysterious, the labels beautiful, the writing bold with names and places she struggled to get her tongue round.

'What's that for?' she asked.

'Well it's not for frying chips,' her mum had said with a laugh.

They visited this stall every other week, and Mum usually bought some slices of garlic sausage. It was passed across in two separate packets. The man worked alone, offered no joke or pleasantries. He would glance at Francesca without smiling.

He never offered her anything.

One Saturday afternoon when she was fifteen, worrying about O-levels, and if she had enough money to buy the latest T. Rex single, Mum produced a list and told her she was on her own with the shopping that week. Dad was at Ewood Park for a league match with the boys and she was suffering with a twisted ankle.

Francesca was beside herself, aghast at the prospect of bartering to get a few pennies knocked off.

Mum saw her face and smiled.

'Just get what's on the list, love,' she said. 'I'm not bothered if you don't get the best price.'

She handed over her purse. 'Don't miss out the olive oil man. He'll give you an extra packet with the meat. It's not important, I know what it is.'

Francesca took the bus alone, wondering if she could make a wheel fall off the trolley on the way back so that it would be consigned to the bin.

She bought her single from the record shop, pretending not to notice some girls from school squashed together in one of the booths. Following the list, she trailed around the market and finally, the only thing left was to visit the olive oil man.

He had a customer, but he nodded to indicate she should wait. As the woman left, he reached for a cloth and wiped his hands.

'A quarter?' he asked.

She looked at the list. It just said salami.

'Yes please.'

She watched him slice the sausage, weigh it and wrap it. From under the counter, he took another packet, and passed it over with the meat.

'Did your mother tell you not to look at that?' he said gruffly.

Francesca shrugged.

'Well,' he said, 'you're nearly an adult, now, and it's for you anyway.'

She paid, pocketed the change, then left. At the bus stop, she joined the queue, and without any hesitation, any thought, pulled the packet out of her coat pocket.

Inside the waxed paper were four ten pound notes.

When Francesca arrived home, she unpacked the shopping, threw the trolley under the stairs and gave her mum the envelope.

'He said it was for me. Why did he say that?'

Her mum stared. 'You've opened it?'

'But he said it was for me.'

She tried to read Mum's face. It was as if her thoughts were tied in a knot that she was struggling to unravel.

'Sit down,' Mum said, 'and I'll tell you, but before I do, remember that your dad and I love you very much.'

Francesca sat on the very edge of the sofa and

placed her hands on her knees. She felt nauseous, her mouth dry, her fingers fizzing with pins and needles.

'I think you know what it means when a man and a woman have an affair,' Mum said.

Francesca waited, alarmed by the creasing in her mother's voice.

'Well, a long time ago, I had an affair.'

Francesca still didn't speak, so her mother said, 'You understand, don't you?'

'It means you ...' she hesitated, 'you went with another man.'

'Yes, I did.'

'What did Dad say?'

'He was angry, upset, we both were. I regretted it and realised it was very wrong.'

'So, what happened?'

Mum hesitated, took a breath.

'We decided to put it behind us. Dad did his best to understand. But I found out I was having a baby because I slept with this other man. That baby was … is, you.'

Traffic passed the house, someone shouted a name, the sound of running feet came and retreated. For a moment, silence wrapped itself around them, a cushion between what had been said and what could happen next.

Francesca realised Mum was crying. Mum never cried.

'So, Dad isn't my real dad?' she asked softly.

'No. Your real father lives in Italy. He sends money for you, always has. His brother is the olive oil man.'

She wiped her face, and sat up. Francesca knew the tears were over.

'It was time to tell you,' Mum said. "There would

never be an easy way to do it.'

Francesca thought about this. She just wanted her world to stay the same and she wasn't sure it could ever be the same, so she started to cry. Mum waited patiently, her arm around her daughter's shoulder.

'Did you love him, my real father?'

'No,' she said. 'I've only ever loved Dad. At the time, it felt like a terrible mistake, but if it hadn't happened, we wouldn't have you, would we? And Dad loves you so much, as much as the boys. He's a very special person, your dad.'

'I know.'

Mum handed her a tissue. 'What happens next is your decision,' she said.

Francesca took a breath, ragged by a final, uneven sob. 'Well I'm not going market shopping again.'

Mum smiled. 'You don't have to. We'll go to the new Tesco. But I didn't mean that when I said you can decide what to do. You could write to your father in Italy?'

Francesca pushed her hair back.

'I could, but not until I've thought about it.'

Emotion surfaced like a bubble and she knew exactly what needed to happen next.

In the hall, she wrenched the trolley out, pulling it into the back yard. She jumped on the wheels, bent the frame, ripped the red tartan plastic from the metal.

Dad and the boys, back from the match, watched in disbelief.

When she knew it was damaged beyond repair, she looked up, her body heaving.

'What's the matter?' Dad said, alarm in his voice.

Her anger vanished. From now on there would be no cheese man or fish man or olive oil man, and no trolley.

She left the mangled frame and wrapped her arms around her dad, the scent of his old duffle coat familiar, a toggle pressing into her cheek, and for the second time that day, her world flipped, then readjusted itself and settled into its rightful place.

'Nothing's the matter, Dad, 'Francesca whispered. 'Nothing at all.'

Brought up in Blackburn, I often went to the market with my mum. As a teenager, I worked on a stall to earn pocket money. The old market hall has been demolished but in my imagination, the feel of it, the smell of food and fish and the echo of Lancashire voices is still vibrant, still present as described in Francesca's story. Thankfully, my mum never had a shopping trolley.

This story was a runner up in the ICB short story competition 2015 and was published in their online anthology.

War and Peace in Lisbon

Liesl turns the package over, reads the address and her maiden name, a name she hasn't used for twenty years. The address still belongs to her parents.

'Well, open it,' Mum says, impatience in her voice. 'I'm intrigued.'

Liesl hesitates. A memory stirs, something doesn't quite slip into place. She pulls away the sticky tape, opens the padded envelope and holds it at eye level to peer inside. Then, careful to reveal only what she wants to reveal, she slides out a paperback book and she knows.

'Oh,' Mum exclaims, touching the book. '*War and Peace*. Is it yours?'

'I think it might have been.'

Liesl opens the front cover and sees handwriting that used to be her style, a style that has changed, matured over the years, but the slope of the ascenders is the same and the letter *a* still doesn't close at the top. Her hands begin to shake so she puts the book down abruptly.

Mum takes it, looks at Liesl's writing, then reads a name written in bolder script.

'Alex Foster. I don't remember anyone called that. Why has he written his name in your book?'

Liesl's bag drops from her shoulder, falling clumsily, contents spilling out. She bends to gather her things, grateful for the brief gift of a moment to collect her thoughts. She lifts herself onto one of the breakfast stools, reaching down to release her work shoes from aching feet. They clatter to the floor. She realises that her mother has asked again about Alex.

'He was at university.' Liesl hears a break in her voice, covering it with a hand to her mouth and a cough. She takes a breath and says with more certainty, 'I think I lent him this book when we were leaving. I put my name and address in the front so he could return it.'

She holds out her hand. She wants the book back.

'Well, why would he write his name above yours if it's not his book? What a cheek, and he's taken a long time to read it,' Mum says with a snort, pushing the book across the shiny surface. Liesl is relieved. Her mother has lost interest now that the parcel is no longer a mystery.

In the garden, Dad and Phil are laughing together, beer glasses in hand, the barbecue smoking with a charred aroma of whatever stuck to the grill last time the weather was warm enough to eat outside. She pushes damp hair from her face. The early evening is hot and humid, the sky, overloaded with cloud. She needs to shower away the working day. Phil catches her gaze and raises his glass.

'Come on love,' he calls. 'It's time you had a drink.'

'We need to pick up Tash, later,' she reminds him. 'I only agreed to let her go if we collected her.'

'You can have one, can't you?'

Liesl smiles at the implication that she will be the one picking up their daughter.

'I'll get a shower and change,' she calls. She casually takes the book and the brown postal bag, grabbing her jacket and shoes. Mum heads for the garden, then turns sharply.

'Is there nothing else with the book,' she asks, 'no note?'

Liesl flips the pages lightly, then looks in the bag

and shakes her head.'

'Nothing.'

'How very odd. I would have expected some sort of apology for keeping it so long. You never mentioned a friend called Alex, or if you did I don't remember.'

Liesl smiles. 'He wasn't a friend, just a guy in my English class.'

'Well, I'd have thought he would have had the courtesy to send a note. It's years since you were at Bristol. He could have ...'

'Mum, could you check Phil has done the salad?' Liesl says. 'He said he would make that pomegranate dressing Dad likes.'

She watches her mother take her drink outside and speak to Phil. He raises his head and says something in her direction, but she can't hear the words. There's a heat spreading from deep within her, a tremble in her lower lip, an unsteady feeling as she walks from the room to the stairs. Reaching for the bannister rail she hesitates, and is almost unbalanced by Phil who catches her around the waist.

'What's up?' he asks. 'Is it the parcel?'

'It's just a book from a friend.'

'Your mum was so curious about it.'

Phil pulls her towards him but she can't return his embrace with hands full of shoes and jacket.

'I wish they weren't here,' she says.

'Hey, don't be like that. They haven't been round for ages. It isn't their fault you've had a bad week, love.'

Liesl drops the shoes and sighs. She's desperate to be alone. 'I know,' she says.

'Go upstairs, have a shower, put on that blue dress I like and come down in a better mood. Take your time, the barbecue will be ages yet. I'll talk cricket with your

Dad and I'll get Tash's school report for your Mum to read – she'll love that.'

He kisses her firmly and directs her up the stairs, collecting the shoes, holding them out so she can take them.

It's cooler in the bedroom. Phil has closed the fine white curtain which billows softly. He has already showered and the air in the room is misted with the familiar scent of him. She undresses, throwing everything over the chair. Pulling her cotton wrap around her, she lies on the bed and reaches for the book and the crumpled envelope. Her fingers investigate a slight raise in the back cover, as if something is inside. Very neatly, two holes have been made in the final page and a hair grip with a butterfly on the end has been pushed through the holes, the butterfly resting against the cover of the book, making an imprint in the card. She breathes out as if trying to empty her head to make room for the memories.

Rain, heat, a city seeming to hunch in a sulk of low cloud and drizzle, grey water greasing the tiled pavements causing more than one person to lose their footing. The Lisbon guidebook suggested a stroll. In fact, words like stroll, amble, relax seemed to leap from the page, but her feet in canvas shoes squeaked with wet, and the relentless drips down her raincoat made two dark, uncomfortable patches on the front of her jeans. Exploring alone was no longer exciting. She was disappointed, irritated, damp.

Choosing a cafe along one side of Rossio Square she sat down, grateful to be under some shelter for the cost of a drink. She had rehearsed the words for coffee with hot milk, but the waiter was as wet as the weather and confirmed her order in perfect, faintly patronising

English. She stowed her umbrella under the table, took the maps and guide books from her bag and began to spread them out.

That morning she had ridden tram 28 with her mother. The narrow vehicle, packed with tourists, had wound its way through the labyrinth of the old town, inching past shops and houses. They had done their best in the Castle of St George, umbrellas up against the driving rain, and enjoyed lunch in a small restaurant, choosing fish as Dad said it was always excellent in this city by the clear, cold waters of the Atlantic. He had left early for a meeting, smart in his suit, tie and polished shoes.

She settled into the chair, pulling the fabric of wet trousers from her skin, shivering despite the humidity. Then she looked up and noticed a man to her left, book in hand, glass of water and coffee cup in front of him. His t-shirt was a peculiar shade of yellow. She tilted her head to read the book title, but before she was sure, he had raised his eyes and looked over.

At the age of nineteen, a year of university behind her, Liesl was beginning to grow into herself, to be comfortable, even a little bit pleased with the person she was. Boys, and men, looked at her appreciatively and she was no longer embarrassed by cat-calling and whistles. In the right mood, she could flash a smile or make a clever retort, if not, she was quite capable of giving a rude gesture. A year ago, just out of school uniform, she would have glanced away. This afternoon, brushing at the wet strands of her dark hair, she smiled.

He had the kind of face that smiled back without even trying; a humorous face, still young, but with strong skin that had lost the pale smoothness of boy. He placed a marker in the book and closed the pages.

Liesl noted the book title.

'War and Peace,' she said. 'I'm impressed.' Then she added, 'I'm sorry, I'm presuming you're English?'

'Have you read it?' he asked.

'No, but it's on my list of books to read. It just looks so…' she hesitated, 'so vast.'

'It's meant to be vast. It isn't a mean little book, it's a great work of fiction.' He said this with a gentle sarcasm underlying the words, as if he were admonishing her for the description.

'I saw the series on television a few years ago,' she said. 'I love the name Natasha, she's a main character, isn't she? If I have a daughter, that's what I'll call her.'

The unsmiling waiter brought her coffee, placing the jug of hot milk on the table with a flourish, as if she had asked for something expensive and rare. She waved away the sugar lumps in a red dish, but he left them anyway. Her fellow customer ordered another coffee and was treated, Liesl thought, with a little more respect.

'I'm Alex,' he said. 'Do you mind if I come over?'

'Please do,' she replied, then, startled by her own enthusiasm said, 'only if I'm not disturbing you.'

'Not at all.' He moved to a chair at her table, bringing with him a wet cagoule, canvas duffel bag, and the book. He put it away, clasped his hands together and Liesl felt his full attention directed at her. It was slightly alarming, but exciting at the same time. She wished she'd ordered a glass of wine.

'So,' Alex said. 'You haven't told me your name.'

'Liesl, as in *I am sixteen going on seventeen,* Liesl.'

He laughed.

'Mum loved that film,' she said. 'And I quite like my name.'

'Only quite?'

'I can't improve on it. It's unusual, but not too different. I sometimes have to spell it or answer questions about whether my parents are Austrian, but I like it. It doesn't shorten very well. Some people call me Lise, but I prefer the whole name.'

'I prefer my shortened name, Alexander is far too long and formal.'

'It's Russian, isn't it? Is there an Alexander in your book?'

'Only the Czar – Alexander the 1st. Hardly inspirational, kept changing his mind.'

'Why are you in Lisbon?' Liesl asked.

'We came for the concert last night. The Rolling Stones,' he said.

'They played here, last night?'

'Yes, you must have seen the posters – Steel Wheels, Urban Jungle Tour.' He indicated the writing on his t-shirt. 'Began last year in America, this is the European leg.'

Liesl looked at the t-shirt and read, 'Lisbon June 10th 1990'.

'Great gig?' she asked.

'Incredible. Best night of my life. Then we got drunk in a bar near our hotel. God knows what time we got in. I seem to remember rather a lot of enthusiastic singing.'

'We?'

'My friend, Linden. He drank too much so he's enjoying being ill in the hotel. I'll prise him from his bed later and we'll go out to eat. We fly home tomorrow. And you?'

'I'm with my parents. Dad's here on business. Mum and I went to the castle on the tram this morning, but she's had an operation on her foot recently so I took her back to the hotel and said I'd go off on my own.'

'She was okay with that?'

'Of course.' Liesl said. 'I left home a year ago.'

'University?'

'Yes.'

'That's not really leaving home, is it? That's just playing at it.'

'Feels real enough to me,' she replied, irritated at his tone.

Alex put a hand to his head and looked up. Water was dripping from a gap in the plastic canopy. 'Come on,' he said, 'let's go inside.'

Liesl's fingers touch the butterfly taking in the delicate silverwork lacing around blues and greens, the end of each wing twisted to a sharp point. Then she pulls the hair grip gently from the book and holds it between her fingers, the memory tugging at her, taking her back to the damp and the wet of Lisbon. Alex's face is still clear, a smile in his eyes, the way his brown hair seemed a little too long to be cool, and she wonders why it has taken him so many years to contact her. He promised he would write, and she waited, and he didn't write, so she stopped waiting, but she didn't forget.

When they entered the bar it seemed full, then Alex noticed a table and he gestured to the waiter to bring their coffees. Liesl wondered where this was leading, but found she was content to follow, to allow herself to be led, to accept whatever was about to unfold. It was as if her parents, university, her boyfriend, Phil, were unreal, and the only reality was this bar and this man.

He asked, 'What are you studying at university?'

'Languages. French and Spanish. It's interesting

how Spanish and Portuguese sound different. Everyone expects them to be similar.'

'I did mathematics,' he said. 'I needed something logical, predictable, something that follows a pattern or a rule.'

'You're a logical person, then?'

Alex smiled slightly. 'Yes, until my emotions kick in, and then it all goes awry.'

Liesl put a hand through her hair and something fell to the floor. 'Oh,' she said, 'it's my hair grip.'

Alex reached down and retrieved it, then turned it between his finger and thumb as if the butterfly was the most interesting thing he had seen for a long time. Liesl waited, but the silence between them was easy.

'It would make a good bookmark,' he remarked holding the hair grip out to her.

'Keep it. Use it in your book.'

Alex took *War and Peace* from his bag, opened it and removed the train ticket which had served as a marker. He slipped the hair grip over a few leaves and closed the book. The butterfly stood out above the pages.

'Perfect,' he said.

'Keep it, please keep it. I should have thought about using it as a bookmark before. Phil bought it for me.'

Alex put the book away and closed his bag. 'Phil?' he said. 'Is he your boyfriend?'

'Yes – well, sort of. We've been good friends in our first year and it's just becoming something more and I'm not sure about it.'

'Not sure? Why not?'

Liesl was surprised at his directness.

'He's a lovely guy, really nice, it's just that he's not

very ... I don't know how to explain it, he's not very definite.' Liesl's voice tailed off.

'Definite?' Alex asked.

'He doesn't seem very sure of himself. He's always asking what I want to do, where I want to go. He likes to take me out, buy me stuff, but needs me to choose it. I wish he'd decide sometimes.'

'Is that indecisive, or does he just want to please you?'

Liesl thought about this. 'I'm not sure, but I wish he was more certain about what he wants from life. He's very good at cricket, played at county level when he was at school and still plays for a local team. The other week when I planned something that clashed with a match, he said he'd miss the match, it wouldn't matter. But I didn't want him to miss the match. I suppose I'm scared of him making me the most important thing in his life.'

'He's scared of losing you.'

'Is he?' Liesl asked. 'I might finish with him when I get back. I'm going away next year, to France for a study year. Perhaps it would be best to tell him.'

Alex took a sip of coffee. 'Be honest with him, and with yourself,' he said. 'Too many couples play games, waste time. Say it as it is. Tell him what you want.'

Liesl looked at him, took in the shape of his face and she wished she was older, wiser, had more life behind her to draw on.

'What about you?' she asked. 'Have you got a girlfriend?'

He hesitated for so long she began to wish the question had never left her thoughts. He seemed to be struggling with something.

'It's complicated,' he said, eventually. 'I have a

crucial decision to make, something that will affect the way I live for the rest of my life, and when I've made up my mind, I intend to stick to it, forever. So, it's essential that it's the right decision.'

'Wow.' Liesl shivered and Alex put his hand on her arm, asking if she was all right. Then his hand was behind her neck, under her hair, and his fingers, certain, definite fingers, caressed her cheek, her jaw, gently moving across her mouth.'

'Can I help?' she whispered. 'Do you want to talk about it?'

Alex took both of her hands in his and looked into her face. 'I can't talk about it,' he said. 'But you are helping. Sitting there looking so young and lovely, you are helping.'

An hour passed. Liesl was entranced. Everything about him was fully formed, mature. Unlike the boys at university, this guy knew what he wanted from life and although he seemed to be at a turning point, she felt he would deal with it properly. This was the sort of man she needed.

They talked about books they had read, films, his work in sales and marketing. Twice, very naturally and very specifically, he reached out a hand to her face, lingering on her cheek, pushing into her hair, behind her neck with great seriousness as if, Lisel thought at the time, he was recalling a distinct memory.

Alex suggested a walk to the River Tagus. As they left the bar, he took her hand and didn't let go until they reached the triumphal arch leading to the Praça do Comércio where the yellow-painted buildings framed the square.

'Same colour as your t-shirt,' she teased.

Alex smiled, but didn't respond. He seemed to be

thinking something through, looking at her, then turning away, gripping her hand, touching every finger in turn. The sun found patches in the cloud and the mosaic pavements of Lisbon steamed, filling the air with an earthy dampness. Liesl knew she had to get back to the hotel.

'I'll walk you back,' Alex said.

'No, I'm fine, it isn't far. Thanks for this afternoon, Alex, I've loved it.'

'I'll get in touch, when we're back in England. Liesl, there's something between us …' He hesitated. 'I can't stop thinking that we didn't meet by chance, did we?'

'I'd love to see you again,' she said.

'Give me your address and phone number. As soon as I've sorted stuff out I'll be in touch.'

Liesl scrabbled in her bag for a pen. She tried writing on an old tram ticket, then a napkin.

'Here.' He took the book with the butterfly hair grip from his bag and opened the first page. Write it here then I'll never lose it.'

She wrote carefully, precisely, because it mattered so much that it was right, and as she wrote, she knew she would finish with Phil and wait for Alex to make his decision and come for her.

By the statue of King José 1, he held her close, his hands moving over her hips and then under her shirt. He placed his thumbs beneath her breasts and she felt desire spread in a warm glow.

This is love, she thought. This is what I want.

Walking away, Liesl experienced a sense of loss almost physical in its intensity. She turned back, but he was a distant figure, head bent, shoulders stooped.

Liesl's fingers reach into the packet and release a cream-coloured card with printed black letters on one side and a photograph on the other. She looks briefly at the photograph, then turns the card and reads the short message.

Linden Rosthorn is devastated to announce the death of his soulmate, friend and life partner, Alexander Foster. Alex fought a long and brave battle with illness, but it took him in the end. He requested a private funeral, expressing a wish for respects to be paid via the website 'just giving' in support of HIV charities.

Under the printed words is a handwritten note that reads; *When we were sorting through Alex's belongings, we found this book and thought that it probably belonged to you.*

Liesl flips the card. She lets the tears brim unchecked. The man in the photograph looks happy. His face is turned directly to the camera and she recognises the shape of it, although the hair is short, and he has a closely trimmed beard. His blue eyes, slightly narrowed against the light, are looking at her.

'So, you made your crucial decision,' she whispers. ''Thank you, Alex, for spending that one, precious day with me in Lisbon before you chose which path to follow.'

She breathes in the familiar scent of Phil's soap and glances over his cricket jumper, shirt and trousers folded neatly on the chair.

'And most of all, thank you for leaving me to choose mine.'

Lisbon is a city full of stories, well worth exploring, whatever the weather. Ride the trams, visit the castle, order coffee in Rossio Square. The waiters are friendly and, unlike Liesl's waiter, never patronising.

On average, the sun shines for 290 days a year. My first visit was, unfortunately, not one of those days.

For my Daughter

I hear the early train slide into the station where the branch line passes the end of the street. The deep barks from a backyard further down the row reverberate against the houses, waking the occupants. He has an accurate internal clock, this dog, but someone needs to set his alarm an hour or so later. The train leaves with a polite swooshing sound. The dog continues to rent apart the early morning until an angry voice curses. A door slams and I listen to the hum of the great industrial town waking up.

I turn over and watch my baby. She is red-cheeked and plump with sleep, her arms relaxed, her legs hidden by the long nightdress. Yesterday she tried to roll over, and with a gentle push from me, found herself on her stomach, a dark head bobbing up to view the world from a new and surprising angle. I laughed aloud at her startled look. She smiled, then cried to be rolled back. They are so helpless at this age. She sleeps where I place her, in our double bed beside me and her night feeds are part of shared nocturnal hours of drowsiness in a damp, close warmth.

The cot my parents bought is in the corner of the room. It is useful for draping clothes that need to air. If my mother asks whether I am using it, I lie.

When I left Richard and returned to England, pregnant, and with nothing, Mum and Dad opened their door to me without question. I had well-rehearsed, if not completely honest, reasons for leaving him. I told them I wanted a child, he didn't, explained he intended to stay in France even though I could see no future for me there, hinted that we had been careless with birth control. They were sad, suggested things could work out, perhaps when Richard saw the baby. I was sad, too, but determined, and when she was born, I knew that I would nurture, care for and provide for my daughter – and I would do it alone.

This puzzled my mother. Looked after by her father and brothers, handed over to my father at 21 to begin a long and happy marriage under his care, she had played the lifelong role of helper, supporter, efficient manager of his household. She was tolerant of his foibles, put his needs before her own and in return, she never had to make decisions or manage money or break out of the circle of comfort she drew around herself. My sister and I, both strong minded girls, found this circle stifling and we challenged her weakness. I asserted myself quietly, stubbornly, Lindsey with anger and frustration that expressed itself in slammed doors and harshly flung words. We left home for college and university at eighteen and never considered the possibility of going back.

I certainly hadn't intended to return at 30, a failed marriage, baby on the way. And despite their kindness and love, I didn't intend to remain.

'Stay with us when the baby's born. Stay for as long as you like,' Mum had pleaded. 'These houses you're looking at aren't in nice areas, love.'

'It's all I can afford,' I said, 'until I can go back to work. Thanks, you've been marvellous, but I can do this on my own.'

She looked at me for a moment, then shook her head. 'Yes, I'm sure you can Joanna, but you don't have to. There's nothing to prove, you know. There's no shame in accepting help.'

'Come with me to look at some properties,' I offered, but my mother shuddered and turned away.

The landlord had smiled bleakly when he saw the baby.

'Thought you were on your own,' he said as he unlocked the house. The front door stuck so he kicked it with his foot.

'Does it matter?' I asked. 'Is the rent more expensive for a baby?'

He shook his head.

'No, but I prefer singles.'

'I am single.'

He shrugged his shoulders and said, 'you might be now, but there'll be some boy sniffing around, won't there? And then there'll be trouble. You girls are all the same.'

I didn't answer, but as he showed me round and we talked a little, he softened. It was basic but clean and newly painted.

'The last one left a mess; bin bags of nappies stinking the place, a freezer full of rotten food because the meter ran out, and she had a dog. The yard was full of crap. Pets aren't allowed.'

'I won't have a pet and I'll look after the house,' I said.

He looked at me. 'Yeah, reckon you might be different. I need a full deposit and a month upfront.'

If he thought this would be a stumbling block, he was wrong. I counted out the cash and put it in his hand.

'You put the deposit in a scheme, don't you?' I asked.

He looked surprised. 'Yes, you'll get a receipt from them. Do you do email?'

'Of course I do.'

From that moment, we seemed to communicate as equals. We swapped details and signed the paperwork, and he became quite cheerful. As he left he said, 'Call me if you need anything, otherwise I'll leave you alone. If I need to visit I'll give you notice.' He looked at me with a sympathetic smile.

'Cute baby,' he said, then he was gone.

I took Jessica from the pram and held her in my arms as we walked through the house and I whispered in her ear, shared my plans, assured her, and myself, that this was the start of our lives together. As soon as I could work again, we would be on our way.

Jessica's lips move in a wry, sideways smile, then she stiffens slightly before sighing and her breathing lengthens into a deeper slumber. She has no sense of the time I spend gazing at her as she sleeps. I know the smooth swell of her cheeks, the fine shape of the pale eyebrows and the line of dark hair high on her forehead. She is perfect.

I hear a car engine in the street and I know it is the 6.30 am lift for Ron next door. In a minute, he will close his front door and scurry to the car, late as usual. As he waits, the driver will keep the motor running, double-parked on this street full of cars. It isn't a bad neighbourhood, but I sense the claustrophobia of too many people in these small houses.

The car door slams, Ron is off to work. He and Margaret have been kind to me. The house is full of their lives; photographs, souvenirs, his collection of brasses, her display of Capodimonte. When she laughs, the sound penetrates the walls. Their television chatters loudly as Ron is deaf, and Margaret plays country music to accompany the chores. I like their noise. It colours my pale, quiet existence with a vibrancy, a reminder that life is rich and full, however small the boundaries seem to be. On the other side, a thin, elderly man lives in silence. I called to introduce myself.

'I'm your new neighbour,' I said. 'Jo.'

He peered at me. 'That's nice.'

'I've a baby, a little girl. I hope you won't mind if she cries.'

'No.'

There was nothing else to say, so he grinned, shrugged his shoulders and closed the door.

I worry about him.

Laying my finger in Jessica's hand she grips lightly, the reflex still strong in sleep. I see Richard in her delicate features, the tiny points on the curve of her ears. He is a neatly made man with dark hair and blue eyes. Perversely, I hope she resembles her father.

We met at college. We were the *sporty* group, walking and climbing at weekends, out until dusk in the summer months, canoeing on the lake, camping wild halfway up a windy fell. When Richard put an arm around me as I shivered in my towel after a midnight swim, I sensed a fitting together of two halves.

College over, we rented a flat and started teaching. I loved my primary school, he hated his position as P.E. teacher. He began to look as grey and miserable as the wet afternoons he spent out on the football pitch with boys who wanted to watch, not play the sport.

We agreed on a gap year and moved to Chamonix where he could ski in the winter and climb in the summer.

'I'll teach English,' I enthused, 'clean chalets, there'll be loads of work in the ski season.'

And I was right, there was plenty of work, but it

was dreary, poorly paid, futureless. The French kids I taught were disinterested, and cleaning chalets after parties of skiers who were ill-mannered, filthy in their habits and completely lacking in any gratitude soon wore me down. When one year became two, then five, I knew I would never find a career in France.

Richard thrived. I was desperate to go home. I talked about starting a family, but he closed his mind to the subject, said he wasn't ready, didn't know if he would ever be ready.

I don't remember the date, the hour, the time when being young and married and in love wasn't enough. One day the mountains and the snow still moved me with their beauty, the next they glowered, stonily, penning me into a life I no longer wanted. The perfect picture of our existence was only that and when it peeled away there was nothing left for me.

I knew exactly what I had to do next.

Sometimes, when I look at Jessica, I feel guilt, but I also feel power. Since human beings walked the earth, women have been made weak by their child-bearing. For millennia, we needed a man's protection.

Yet in the last few seconds of mankind's time line, the balance has finally tipped in our favour. We can decide to bear a child or to remain childless. We don't even need a man, only his seed, and, more crucially, a woman can have a child when she chooses to and remain alone.

The thought of that power, and how I used it, excites me. The guilt I carry will never fade, but carry it I shall, for my pride, my independence and for my daughter.

The mother in this story is Jo, who develops into an independent, career-minded headteacher. She is at a crossroads in the novel **Holding On Letting Go**. *Bizarrely, although I created her, she was hard to get to know. I wrote this short story in the first person to try and understand an important episode in her earlier life which continues to shape her future.*

I think it worked.

A Square of Light

I used to live a life of curves; the rump of a hill, thunder clouds piling up in a hot sky, my wife's hip as she lies facing me, the line of her body smooth under the sheet. Nature shows a discomfort with right angles and straight lines, yet men will seek to fashion them still. The mason reaches for a rock, roughly formed, unique. He removes its identity with his chipping and tapping and is only satisfied when it is like the others he has shaped.

There are no curves in my cell. It is square-based, high-walled with rectangular stones. This Saracen builder was indeed diligent. He left few awkward edges, although I found them all when I scrutinised the intimate corners of my world. Sometimes, in desperation for softness, I hurl my blanket across the floor and watch the fabric settle in folds and creases. I see peaks and valleys, river courses, a flat stretch of water, and I think of home.

But I have a gift – the gift of an empty square, and through the space created by right angles and four straight sides, light enters. I cannot reach my square, but I devise the sides to be the length of my arm, elbow to fingertip. Out there, I imagine the beams of an alien sun creating a broad sweep, catching the shiny surfaces; sparkles on running water, flashes of brilliance when a sword is lifted high or a precious jewel shines on a woman's breast. These things can be seen by everyone, but my square of light is mine and I am blessed because it is rich and intense and solely for me.

It looks west. In the morning, it admits a softness when grey dawn creeps in. If the sky is clear, my light is warm and yellow, paler when it is cloudy, almost white when the moon deflects the rays of the unsleeping sun. As day lengthens, so does my light. It may be framed with regular sides and corners, but the arc of the sun creates subtle changes on the opposing wall. Each evening I wait for a particular moment when the square becomes perfect. Catching my breath, I watch it form, then slip into irregularity. I follow its rise up the wall, as it expresses for me the most glorious, most intense shades, before fading into darkness.

Then, I scratch another mark on the floor.

I came to this land to serve my Lord and he has granted me a peace I would never have known if I had stayed by the hearth and grown old with the dogs licking my fingers and my children tumbling around me.

They have taken everything, left only the rags that cover my bones. But in taking everything, they have opened my eyes to something priceless because it is rationed, contained, yet delivered unfailingly through an open and empty stone square.

My square, my light.

TSS Flash Fiction Competition (winter, 2016)
1st Place.

The judge loved this piece and placed it in the Best of the Best in 2019. He said it was; A sublime Flash Fiction that was absolutely pitch-perfect in tone and pace. It offered the raw, painful details within a beautiful poetry that was rhythmic, but concise, offering a startlingly imaginative perspective that absolutely caught the mystery of the narrator's loss and wonder.

My Father

I stand in the ancient porch, the chill of flagstones seeping through my silk pumps. The vicar hovers, my sister Julia in her aqua-blue bridesmaid's dress peeps around the door to check the guests over.

'David looks nervous,' she whispers, 'he can't keep still.'

I think about the man who is to be my husband. Perversely I can't help feeling a little pleased to be the cause of his nerves. I hold this moment and it feels good.

'Ready?' asks the vicar. He's a kind man. He talked us through our vows, started to make the case for including the word *obey*, flinched at my derision, and David's snort of laughter. Meeting over, he took us to the pub and we bought him a pint.

He pushes the double doors wide open. The pews look full. I can see the dark green of Mum's tight little hat. As another guest shakes her head, feathers flutter and, nearby, a wide-brimmed navy circle stands out above blond hair.

'Leisurely,' he says. I meet the twinkle in his eye with a confident smile. 'Let them take a moment to look at you.' He touches my arm and leans towards me, sympathy, which I don't need, in his expression.

Julia takes her place and waits, flowers clasped demurely. Later, she will get drunk and dance erratically and tell me I'm her favourite sister.

The clergyman wafts down the aisle, his snowy cassock billowing. He motions the congregation to stand and I hear the first optimistic notes of the *Wedding March.*

I tilt my chin, straighten my shoulders and begin to walk.

I don't remember the exact day I came to understand my father, to know he would never hug me, read to me, give my achievements any more than a cursory glance. I accepted his brusque tones and his sarcasm, knew to avoid his outstretched palm when Mum detailed my misdemeanors. We learned to keep our distance. If he was travelling with his job, we ran circles around Mum and I ruled the roost.

At thirteen, I was a self-opinionated teenager, struggling with my emotions, forever polishing the veneer that hid them. One day, we came home from school to find Mum in the backyard crying so hard she couldn't speak, each sob a huge whooping intake of air, animal-like, exhausting. We put our arms around her. I sent Julia for a neighbour.

Mrs Winter supported my mother inside, sat her in a chair and told me to put the kettle on and make tea.

'Plenty of sugar, love,' she said.

I listened. Heard the word, *gone*, then, *left me*. My heart skipped.

As Mum sank into despair and succumbed to a lethargy that confined her to bed for weeks, Julia and I contemplated the prospect of our lives without the dark shadow he had thrown over us.

'He isn't coming back? You're sure?' I asked, over and over again.

As the weeks became a month, and the months lengthened into a year, we dared to hope, to relax into a future without him. As Mum diminished, we grew and the best part was that I was in charge. When the bills piled up, I paid them. If a light bulb blew, I changed it, and when the sink blocked or a shelf fell down, I called the kindly Mr Winter in, watched what he did and knew that the next time it happened, I could do it myself.

Mum never recovered, but she stopped weeping. She cared for us, cooked, cleaned, took up a part-time job, but the lights had gone out. Her smiles were forced, her occasional laughter, nervous, her figure, diminished. Without a man, there was nothing to give her definition. I promised myself I would never be like her, I would grab life and face every challenge on my own.

At eighteen, I left home to go to university. My bags packed and waiting in the hall, I sat with Mum in the kitchen drinking tea. September had been glorious, the days still warm and I had camped out with friends in those precious few weeks before we all went our separate ways.

'Julia will miss you,' she said.

'I can come home at weekends, it isn't far,' I replied, knowing that I almost certainly wouldn't.

'You might find a boyfriend.'

'I'm not looking for one.'

The pause became awkward, then she raised her hands to her face and I realised she was crying.

'Mum.'

'I've made such a mess of my life,' she managed to say.

'How?'

'Losing your dad.'

'Losing him? He walked out on us, you didn't lose him.'

She took out the screwed-up hanky that was always pushed in her sleeve and wiped her eyes.

'I lost him the day I knew I was having a baby.'

Realisation dawned.

'Me?'

'Yes, you.'

She got up abruptly and went to the back door, leaning on the frame, gazing towards the little yard. I looked at her knee-length skirt and jersey and wondered why she never wore trousers or a dress or a pair of dungarees in electric blue. Everything seemed chosen to camouflage her so effectively no one would notice she was there. She turned and came back to the table.

'He never wanted kids,' she said.

'I gathered that.'

'He thought you took me away from him. He was a good husband.'

I was incensed. 'And a terrible father.'

'It wasn't his fault – it was mine.'

'Bloody hell, Mum, it takes two to make a baby,' I threw at her.

'He wanted you adopted, but I couldn't do it,' she said. 'I promised him it wouldn't change things, but it did, of course it did.'

Adopted – better all round, placed in a home where both parents wanted us, probably desperately. I might have had a father who could love his children and his wife at the same time. Love shouldn't be finite. It expands, encompasses the whole family, stretches like bread dough, and then you just make some more.

I had to ask, 'but you had a second child?'

'I did it for you, so you'd have a friend. I persuaded him another one would mean you'd have each other and, after a few years, he'd have me again. I was so glad it was a girl.'

I took the mugs and went to the sink, rinsing them under the tap. Then I ran cool water over my wrists as I contemplated her words, wondered why she had never said any of this before. A wave of regret covered me, for us and for her. At forty-two she felt her life was a mess and all because a man had put his selfish needs before anything else.

'He was a bastard,' I said.

'He loved me.'

'He hated us. How can you hate your own children? And then he left you.'

'He really loved me,' she repeated, 'and he'll come back, he said he would.'

'And you believed him?'

'Of course.'

I told her she was deluding herself, made her promise never to let him in, especially if she and Julia were alone.

She agreed, but I wasn't convinced.

I loved university, but after a wild first year, the popular crowd, so interesting at first, began to irritate me with their languor, their feigned disdain of student life. I finished a pointless relationship with a guy who had been entertaining, but thought far too much of himself, spent the summer working and returned in the autumn to share a flat with two mature students.

On a freezing November night, David walked me home from the bar. He took my hand and placed it in his pocket, a simple act that melted a tiny corner of my independence. He spent the next few weeks seeking me out, his shyness hiding a strength of character. I became used to an apologetic look becoming a hopeful smile in my direction, something shared, although at first, I wasn't sure what it was.

That summer, we took a tent and a primus stove and hiked the coastal paths in Cornwall. The weather was sultry, every day bathed in sunshine. One night we pitched by a cove that could only be reached on foot. He dared me to swim naked, admitting later he knew I would do it. I stripped off without a second thought and headed for the sea, turning to flash a deliberate, seductive glance in his direction, wondering if he would join in. I decided that if he did, I would marry him.

A week later, we visited his parents, who were very sweet. His mother insisted we had separate rooms – for heaven's sake, what did she think we were doing in a two-man tent? I teased him, pretended to be grateful she was giving me a couple of nights off and rejected his suggestion that he sneaked into my room as his parents slept.

'You quite wore me out with all your demands last week,' I said.

'I don't remember any complaints from you,' was his reply.

'I wouldn't have dared,' I insisted, with all the innocence I could muster. 'I was completely at your mercy.'

In the early hours, when I felt him push me across the narrow bed, his desire evident, I shivered with the power I had to arouse him and the strength he had to hold me. We were equals in everything, and I was learning to let him look after me, to hand over some part of myself because doing so would never be a threat.

The congregation turn as I walk down the aisle. There are smiles of joy, delight, and from some, sympathy that I am a lone figure in my bridal gown. Uncle Ted would have walked with me, Mr Winter offered, David's father suggested he could give me away. Much to my mother's disgust, I declined them all.

'I'll be like Maria,' I announced.

'Maria who?'

'Maria Von Trapp. There was no-one to give her away, she was an orphan. The Mother Superior couldn't do it, could she? She walks down that long, long aisle alone. I want to do the same.'

Halfway and I see David turn. The shy smile hasn't changed. He brushes fingers through his dark hair, comes to meet me. It's no surprise. We have rehearsed this with the vicar. There is some polite murmuring, a whisper of incredulity. He takes my hand, kisses my cheek and we finish the wedding march together, a gasp of delight rippling around the church.

We are welcomed and the service begins, old familiar words, this time for me, for us.

I start at the slam of a door. The vicar looks over our heads to the back of the church, surprise in his face. My body stiffens. David grips my hand, glances over his shoulder. He puts his lips to my ear and I wonder if I can stay on my feet as anxiety spreads from my gut. The dampness in his whisper makes me shiver.

'The wind,' he says, 'it must have slammed the door.'

I close my eyes, collect my thoughts, breathe.

Of course it was the wind – it couldn't have been anything else.

In ***Walking Alone****, David and Helen Richards celebrate the wedding of their elder daughter and Helen recalls their own wedding more than 30 years ago. Having a father who walked out on the family shaped Helen from an early age. Yet her strength of character and poise in her professional life hide an emotional fragility which contributes to the issues in her marriage.*

Her father never returns.

Colouring in for the Middle-aged Woman

Anna

It was a hair appointment in a traditional salon just off the high street, where Anna didn't feel intimidated by staff who spoke in words she struggled to understand, or scared her with a defiance of tattoos and piercings.

The stylist rambled on, asked about her daughter, Ellie, and the boys. As she combed out the wet strands of freshly-coloured hair, a shade lighter this time, Anna glanced at herself in the mirror. Her father's green eyes, slightly oriental in shape, looked back at her. But today there was something else, a glimpse of a face both distant yet familiar.

She turned her head slightly and as the light caught her chin, realised that the visage looking back bore more than a vague resemblance to Aunt Maggie. Her sharp intake of breath went unnoticed as Louise reached for the scissors, asking how much to cut, exclaiming how quickly it had grown and how lucky she was at her age to have such thick hair. But Anna wasn't listening, she was remembering – Aunt Maggie, thin-faced, forever old, mouth drooping in disapproval. Panic rose, then squashed itself into a tight, screwed-up ball that she knew would drain all colour from her mood leaving a washed-out, depressing greyness.

A few weeks ago, the counsellor had suggested using colours.

'Is this a new approach for middle-aged women who can't cope?' Anna had asked, aware that her sarcasm bordered on rudeness.

'No, not at all,' Maureen said, her speech slow, deliberate in tone, as if talking to a small, uncomprehending child. 'It's something I devised years ago to help me, and it's helped other women get through this stage in their lives.'

Anna sighed, forced a smile.

'Does it work?'

'Sort of. When I look back over a week and see more blues and greens, it gives me some confidence that I can get through the grey.'

'Or black,' Anna said.

'Not much of that.'

For fuck's sake, no black?

Anna would never have said it aloud, but she was using the *f* word more and more in her head. One day she would shock her husband and pronounce it, emphasis on the *ck* which was such a satisfactory ending to an expletive.

Maureen looked directly at her, eyebrows raised.

'Black,' she continued, 'is for days when you can't even get out of bed.'

So Anna took the idea and thought she would try it. She printed out a calendar, and began to colour in the days: shades of soft, pencil grey, reds when anger and frustration surged, green for neutral, clear, pale blue for organised thinking then yellow for the occasional joyous, energised days when she felt she could tackle anything.

But she realised that it wasn't enough to colour in a whole block for each day. Some mornings emerged in a shroud of grey, then became red and could fade to green or back to grey. She started to mix the colours, sometimes using two or three pencil crayons together for an overlapping of moods. For Christmas, Andrew bought her an adult colouring book and thought he was, for once, being clever.

'I don't like colouring in patterns,' she said. He looked hurt and confused at the same time. Anna regretted her words. In fact, the disappointment in his face made her turn away to blink back ridiculous tears. So she thanked him and said she would give it a go and she exclaimed at the pretty designs. He left her to it. She went back to the chart.

She realised that she needed purple, not a colour she had ever favoured, but with a predominance of crimson, it was voluptuous, sexy. It encompassed feelings that were surprising her after years of being too tired and weary at the end of a day at work. A purple flush swept over her in the morning, before supper, when Andrew was there and when he wasn't.

Her calendar became a beautiful thing. The black crayon remained sharp-tipped. I would never have stayed in bed, Anna thought to herself.

She left the salon, glancing at the market clock. She was meeting her husband in half an hour for another house viewing, and this one was important. The image of her Aunt, who had never married, always did exactly as she wanted and always got what she wanted, was strong. Anna set her shoulders, lifted her chin and strode across the square to Finch and Forgham Solicitors to pick up the keys. Seeing Aunt Maggie in the mirror was colouring the day steely grey; grey for strength, for resolve, with a lining of silver, like storm clouds at the end of a hot day in August.

It was a short, brisk walk from the town centre. Andrew met her at the gate. She read his body language; hands deep in trouser pockets, mouth a straight line.

She sensed a challenge. Taking his arm, Anna reached up for a kiss, told him she loved him and had missed him since they parted at breakfast when he had been reluctant to come along for the viewing. He faced her.

'We said no work, no renovation. We said we'd had enough of all that. This place obviously needs gutting,' he protested.

Along the garden path, away from the road, there was peace and a sense of time long passed. The leaded windows caught the sun and glinted with a richness of colour. She put the key in the lock. It turned easily, although the door took the full weight of her hip and shoulder to open. He stood back before following her inside.

'I think,' she said carefully, 'that you'll have to use your imagination with this one and see how we can make it work for us.'

He shrugged and scratched his head, looking completely unconvinced as she closed the door behind them. For a moment she hesitated, then put the key back in the lock and turned it.

'Just in case,' she said. 'They've been very trusting giving us the keys. We wouldn't want anyone wandering in, would we?'

Low sunshine warmed the oak floors and caught the faded paintwork, mellowing the house with warmth and light, brush-stroking some yellow across Anna's mood. There was no furniture, just a few broken pieces carelessly abandoned. Andrew said little as they toured the rooms but she ignored his grunts, and the grey knot inside her began to loosen. She felt a stirring below her rib cage that suggested possibility, opportunity. Finally, she opened the door to the master bedroom. Against the backdrop of ancient wallpaper stood a four-poster bed in carved oak, beautifully draped. She pretended to consult the brochure and took a deep breath.

'And this,' she announced,' is included.'

She stepped towards the bed and sat on the edge of the mattress. Drawing up her legs, she lay back, glancing at him through a thick strand of hair. She took the strand and pushed it behind her ear. At last she saw the glimmer of a smile, a break in the frosty stare, a relaxing of the shoulders beneath his sharply-tailored jacket.

He grinned.

Leaning against one of the posts, he touched the wood, then the fabric. He said, 'You look so like Ellie.'

Anna almost replied, *Ellie? Not Aunt Maggie?*

She clambered across and knelt up to loosen his tie, pulling the neatly tucked shirt from his belt, slipping her hands behind his back.

'So,' she said. 'Have you been using your imagination as I told you, or do you need some help?'

She pulled him down beside her. When he took her hand, she was confident she could win him over. She looked up at the ceiling, which had been painted a faded, yet quite unmistakable shade of purple. Then she closed her eyes and allowed the colour to seep through her senses.

Andrew

He left the office with an overwhelming feeling of things remaining unfinished in a pointless, unnecessary way. This viewing was a waste of time. He'd seen the artful photographs and read the text – well they didn't fool him. As far as he was concerned, it was another emotional whim of Anna's. She was both concerning and annoying him.

Last month he had sat with her in the doctor's consulting room and felt awkward, embarrassed as she described her anger, her fatigue, the hopeless feelings which descended without warning and covered her every thought with a dark, suffocating misery. He knew she was struggling to sleep, to eat normally, to accept the changes in her face and her body, but he was ageing too. His joints creaked, his hair was grey, almost white in places and he wasn't making such a fuss about it. The doctor suggested counselling and he blurted out, 'Do we pay for that?' immediately regretting his words as both his wife and the medic turned to stare at him.

'Not that it matters,' he muttered. 'The cost isn't important.'

What he really wanted was Anna out of the room, then he could tell the doctor what effect the so-called *change of life* was having on him. It was like living with a different woman each day. She was unpredictable, sometimes childishly exuberant, then silent. She would reach for him under the duvet, demanding intimacy and passion, and then, as if he hadn't done enough, would turn her back and shut him out.

He wanted his wife as she used to be, pills, potions, counselling – whatever it took. He'd had enough of trying to comfort her when she bought towels of the wrong shade, or came off the phone to one of the children, grieving the distances between them, enough of anticipating her moods and tantrums. At times, he wished she was back at work because work provided an excuse for her behaviour; the reason she couldn't always control herself. Her job had been stressful, it drained her, left her emotionally vulnerable and tired, but work was no longer part of the picture. Unconsciously, Andrew was afraid to delve too deeply into the reasons Anna still seemed to be struggling with life as that would involve looking a little more closely at himself.

She came home from the first and only session of counselling with nothing more useful than some stuff about colouring in a chart. He listened, bemused, but determined to be encouraging.

'Didn't the doctor suggest taking up a new hobby, a sport?' He leant on the table to look more closely at what she was doing. 'Lots of women take up golf when they're older. You could come to the club with me.'

She raised her eyebrows, selected another crayon, a red one, and looked at him as if she would like to push it, very hard, into the back of his hand.

'Boxing,' she said. 'I rather fancy boxing.'

He snorted. She flung the crayons into the tin and shut the lid with a sharp snap.

She'd never decide to take up boxing, he thought. His usually calm, deliberately thoughtful wife, who had held down an important and demanding job before retiring, was now finding it hard to make up her mind about anything.

'You choose,' she said on a number of occasions. 'I'm having an orange day today. I can't even decide between tea or coffee.'

Then there was the colouring book he bought her for Christmas, with a bottle of her favourite perfume, of course. He thought she would be pleased, but his smugness at having an original idea for once had been short-lived. When she said she didn't like colouring in, he was too baffled to point out that she seemed to do little else these days.

Well, as far as the new house was concerned, he would be making the decisions. They only needed two bedrooms – he didn't want the kids thinking they could come back. A place near the town centre would be ideal with a small patio or yard. No major work, although a bit of decorating could be arranged. It was a straightforward decision, black and white, no shades of grey.

The first thing he noticed at the house was the overgrown box hedge around the tangled garden and the empty rusted hinges where a gate should have been. He was determined to humour her, but also put his foot down about this one. Retiring next year, it was the golf course, not Wednesdays (discount day for the over sixties) in the DIY superstore that he had in mind. He crossed the threshold, hands in pockets, coins jingling disinterestedly.

'Look at the windows catching the sun,' he heard her say. 'They still have the original leaded lights.'

'Draughty,' he replied. 'They'll cost a fortune to replace.' He started to add up some figures, then stopped himself. If they weren't buying this wreck, why bother? And she certainly wouldn't get around him by going all girly. Then she'd had the nerve to tell him to use his imagination.

They stepped inside. He watched his wife close and then lock the front door, muttering something about agents and trust, although he couldn't see why anyone would want to break in. For God's sake, even squatters would turn around and leave in disgust.

There was dust everywhere, curtains dangled raggedly and hideous wallpaper prints seemed to darken the rooms, despite the sunshine.

'Can you believe this kitchen?' he gasped. 'There's

nothing here except a sink.' Her smile irritated him.

'Oh come on, you're not serious Anna? This house is out of the question. I can't see us living here.'

The staircase felt spongy, probably rotten. He muttered under his breath at the uneven steps and a carpet that was escaping the stair rods, and swore as a loose floorboard on the landing caught his toe. Once again, his wife just smiled.

The master bedroom was huge. He gaped at the four-poster bed, obviously antique, worth a bit. Anna looked at the agent's description and Andrew knew exactly what she was going to say before she said it. It wouldn't make any difference, and the sooner he got her out of this house and back to reality, the better. She looked at him, her eyebrows raised, sat on the bed and bounced lightly. He couldn't help smiling as she flung herself back on the dusty mattress cover. Married for thirty-five years and she could still behave like a teenager.

Andrew sighed. The taught elastic inside his head slackened and, for a moment, all he knew was how much he loved her. Perhaps this house would provide some focus, an outlet for the frustration she seemed unable to channel. It might take her mind off the bloody colouring in and get her thinking about tins of paint and wallpaper and fabrics.

His hands touched the drapes. The fabric felt heavy, strangely opulent in this drab, colourless place.

'You look so like Ellie,' he said, the thought becoming words rather unexpectedly. She opened her mouth as if to challenge this, then smiled. He knew what game she was playing as she loosened his shirt and tie and pulled him down beside her. Well, he could play too. He took her hand. She was right, the bed was really something. She was gazing at the ceiling, a smile brightening her face with a glimpse of youth. He looked up but his eyes were drawn to a creeping patch of damp. Stroking her soft, smooth hair, he pushed a hand beneath her blouse. Imagination she'd said? He could still show her plenty of that.

'What an odd colour,' he remarked, following her upward glance. 'Is it lilac, mauve?'

'Purple,' she said. 'Gorgeous shade, don't you think?'

'You don't like purple.'

She sighed, touched his face with her hand and whispered in his ear.

'I do now.'

Anna is one of my favourite characters. She is tackling the confusion many women feel in their 50s and 60 as their bodies change and a life of working and bringing up children reaches an end.

I am unsure about whether they will buy the house, but they will, without doubt, settle into a retirement that suits them both!

Frozen

The furred hood is trapped under the strap of her bag. She gives up, allowing snow to settle on her hair. The flakes are hypnotic, falling obliquely, felting a rough blanket to be carelessly thrown across the village in gentle folds. She thrusts her hands in deep pockets, breathes slices of cold air and hears the squeaking of her footsteps.

The meeting finished late. She wonders what mood her husband will be in when she arrives home, their harsh words at breakfast forgotten as she took on the day. Now she remembers.

'I want you back,' he said before she left for work. 'All of you. I've shared you with that job for too long.'

She imagines walking on past their house, beyond the village, thinking only where to place her feet in the snow, one foot in front of the other, each print of her boot a new shape, gently filled in. Soon, there would be no trace.

A dark figure is there on the pavement. She is startled, loses her balance. He grabs her arm.

'I wondered where you'd got to?' he says, steadying her.

She gasps. 'You frightened me.'

He takes her hand. 'No gloves?'

'No.'

He untangles her hood from the strap and pulls it over her head, then he covers her hand and places it in his warm, gritty pocket.

The scene is strange, unreal. Without warning, a huge swell of emotion spreads like a cold flush. Her eyes fill with tears, then with one blink, they are streaming down her face, falling on the front of her coat with the melting snowflakes. As they reach the front door, he turns to unlock and she swipes at the tears with her sleeve.

In the hallway, he looks at her as she throws off her hood. The smell of cooking, which should be welcoming, only serves to tense her stomach. Conflict looms.

'Are you all right, love?'

She reaches for a tissue to wipe her face. She knows she should thank him for coming to meet her, be grateful he isn't annoyed that she is late again, let him look after her. Instead she passes the wet coat and says, 'Of course I am, don't fuss. I need to warm up.'

She sees him turn away, shoulders slumped, and she wonders where all the energy for their marriage has gone and why she can't tell him how she feels. It's as if part of her has hibernated. If she lets go of the work that gives her status, control, the rest will follow into that long grey sleep called retirement.

She watches her husband hang up the coats. It's still a surprise not to see brightly coloured anoraks, snowsuits, red wellies, a lone glove or sock abandoned on the floor, its owner too busy to pair it up.

Only their sombre outdoor wear and two well behaved rows of boots and shoes remain.

The passing of years can move us all to sadness. Helen is struggling to envisage a purposeful existence as retirement looms and she feels increasingly more distant from her husband of 30 years. Although the couple in this short story are un-named, they are Helen and David in the novel, ***Walking Apart***.

Catching the Spark

Silence hangs against the curtain of city noise. He snatches a breath, then he slaps me, hands heavy, the palms, flat. His blows are not to damage. He is angry and hurt. I have let him down.

People stare, some smirk, most walk on.

'You bitch,' he shouts. 'Why now?'

The words fragment with emotion and I know the rage will abate. We've shared much over the years, the two of us. I've nested his steamed-up love-making, listened to his talk, puffed out in blue shreds of smoke, provided shelter in lay-bys as he slept out the haze of alcohol. When his mother passed away, we drove to Scotland in a night, returning to London the next morning a little worn, a little older.

The weight of him has changed. He uses his feet on my pedals differently now, the actions deliberate and smooth, the movements practised. I have to admit, he keeps me in good form, choosing to hand me to the experts if part of me fails. We no longer struggle on; he ensures I am fixed.

Last week, a smart-suited friend with cardboard coffee in hand, sat beside him. Hot liquid splashed my dashboard.

'No cup holder, mate?'

Smart Suit slagged me off – my age, my lack of *toys,* my sluggishness. When this so-called friend got out, slamming the door, we pulled away in silence. He lit a cigarette, and I knew he was thinking.

I was taken to a place of smug, well-behaved vehicles. Feet kicked my tyres and hands violated my hidden places. The talk was breathy, punctuated with sighs and a sucking of air to be exhaled in slow whistles.

He dreamed of speed and climate control and surround sound, so I imagined dirt and rust and a furring of vital parts.

When he cleared out my glove box, I knew the time had come. I could have refused to start outside the flat. Far more effective to putter and stall on the way, traffic piling up behind us, the grey sky threatening rain. His rage was expected, his petulance typical.

Horns blast. Angry words rent the air. He ignores them. His body relaxes into my leather seat. He whispers, 'It's as if you know.'

He touches the keys dangling from the ignition.

'Last chance,' he says. 'Start on one, and we continue to the showroom, on two, we turn around and head home. Anything else and I ring the scrappers.'

We've played this game before. It used to be a pair of dice hanging from the mirror, tossed onto the passenger seat. Evens he'd ditch the girl, odds we'd wait all night outside her house, that sort of thing. It was the dice that sent us to Scotland.

First turn – I rattle over, once, twice, then die.

He sighs, tightens his grip on the ignition key, hope greasing his fingers.

In my carburettor the grit shifts, something loosens and clears.

I wait to catch the spark.

Older cars have character – little quirks that need careful handling – irritating and endearing in equal measure.

Sometimes we name a car, talk to it, feel a genuine sadness when the final day arrives and we leave it at a garage, guiltily driving away in a newer vehicle.

The make, model and colour of this car was defined as I wrote the short story, but such details have deliberately been left to the imagination of the reader.

Fell Walkers

A fretful, surprising wind blew in sudden gusts, unbalancing the fell walkers. It tugged at loose straps on rucksacks, coats, hair, flattening clothes against their bodies. Anxious to leave the summit, the group hurried on but he found a sheltered corner where the two of them rested against a rock, laughing and breathless.

She said, 'I'm happy when I'm with you. You're kind, thoughtful, clever, and when you find these little tracks and know exactly which way to go, I just ...' she hesitated, felt the weight of the words; they could change everything in a moment. 'I just feel safe.'

She could have said, 'loved', but she didn't. She glanced at him, wished he would reach out and take her hand, hold it, only that.

As they left their shelter, the fretful wind, determined to have its say, took a deep rasping breath and blasted them with a splatter of stinging sleet. She lost her balance. He reached to steady her. Then, he was holding her hand.

Once she was upright they should have let go, but she held on down the track, until they reached the kissing gate. She slipped through first, then she turned to look at him, her hair roughly blown, her cheeks glowing. He pushed her gently against the fence and kissed her.

Winter lost its grip, and the emerging spring gave her senses a sharpness. They were meeting for a walk so she prepared a sandwich lunch, buttering bread, laying ham in thick slices. She felt the rough grain of the loaf, caught the smoky smell of the meat, and when she licked the smear of mustard from her fingers it was sharp and hot across her tongue.

He was there when she arrived, studying the map. She crossed the car park and stood in front of him until he pulled her close, his hands connecting with bare skin under the back of her shirt.

'Lovely,' she said. 'I've missed you.'

He kissed her, and she wondered, did he still kiss his wife with passion, touch her skin like this? Had they made love the previous night?

I don't need to know, she thought. This is today and he's with me.

The weather turned in the last hour of the walk and they made a quick dash to the cars. She sat under the rear door of his hatchback as he took the muddy boots from her wet feet.

'Leave them when you get home,' he said. 'I'll clean them for you.'

'Come and do them now,' she suggested. 'Surely your wife won't be home yet.'

'Actually,' he said, 'she's away until tomorrow.'

'Overnight?' She held her breath.

'Yes.'

'Come to my place, I'll cook a meal for us.'

She watched his face, saw the possibilities sink in.

'Yes,' he said. 'I would really like that.'

She wanted to say that *really like* sounded as if she was offering to open a box of chocolates. She kissed him on the cheek and said, 'I'll see you later.'

At home, she showered. I want him forever, she thought, but I can't have him. He'll go back to playing happy families because he's a good man and this deception is so alien to him.

She stood in front of the mirror, towelling her hair,

then she shrugged off her robe. She wished she was slimmer, taller, less rounded. She turned sideways, pleased at the shape of her breasts, not so pleased at the curve of her stomach. She thought about his thin wife. A shiver had her reaching for the robe.

She chose clothes with care; black jeans and a blue satin shirt with pearl buttons, velvet pumps. Her hands shook as she applied make-up and selected perfume.

The task of putting a meal together calmed her and she was sliding the dish into the oven when she heard a knock. He was there, clean shaven, hair slightly damp. He kissed her on the mouth.

In the rear porch, he set to work on the boots. She watched him. His hands were deft with the stiff brush and she felt desire for this man as he carried out the simple task for her.

Yet there was something unsure in his movements.

'I'll stay to eat,' he said as he washed his hands, 'but I can't leave too late.'

So, he had decided that things had gone far enough.

She said, 'Why have you come back?'

He turned from the sink. 'Because you asked me. Because I want to spend the evening with you.'

'Is that all?'

The implication was clear.

'No. I've thought that eating together might not be the only thing we would do this evening.'

She felt a tightness in her stomach; a grip of something pleasurable, uncertain.

She passed the towel and said, 'Where is this going? I love our time together, I love feeling your hands on me, and I've desperately wanted more, but we'll never have anything better than a secretive, *meeting once a week* kind of relationship, will we?'

'You need to find a single guy,' he said uncomfortably. 'You don't need me.'

Within a minute he could be gone.

'I do need you,' she said.

They poured wine, took their glasses into the lounge and sat without speaking. She put her glass down, and moved to sit closer to him, relieved when he put his arm around her shoulders.

'I need a partner,' she said, 'I'm no good on my own, and one day I'll find someone, but it won't be you.'

'Then why ..?'

'I have to start somewhere. I'm scared. I was married for 25 years, but it was dilute, lacking any passion. I know nothing about being in love.'

'Then why start with me?'

'I've fallen for you. But it's a sort of practice falling in love. With your wife, you have a past and a future. You and I, we need each other now.'

She breathed in his closeness.

'So,' she said, 'if you stay the night, it's fine. It's a separate thing, just you and I doing something we want to do tonight.'

There was a pause. She thought, how can I bear it if he says no?

He lifted his arm, almost roughly. She thought he was angry but he stood up, grasped her hand and pulled her to her feet.

He looked at her. 'You're sure?'

'Quite sure,' she said, 'but I'm frightened. I don't know what to do. I'm scared I'll be a disappointment.'

'It's a first for me, too,' he said.

'Of course – a first for both of us.'

In her bedroom, she moved clothes from the bed, pushed shoes under a chair, closed the curtains. She turned to him.

'Lie down,' he said softly.

She lay on the bed, her pulse racing. He sat beside her, slipped the pumps from her feet.

'Don't think,' he said. 'Relax. Try and tell me what works for you.'

Suddenly she was petrified. 'I've forgotten what works. I don't know if I ever knew.' She could hear the panic.

'Don't worry,' he said, 'we'll find out.'

She gave him a nervous smile.

'Shall I get undressed?'

'Absolutely not,' he said, his fingers touching the pearl buttons. 'That's definitely my job.'

There was no disappointment. He was unhurried, gentle, knew what she needed. Once, he stopped, lay very still, his face almost touching hers and told her she was beautiful. When it was over, he wrapped himself around her. She wanted to say thank you, but that seemed wrong, so she said nothing. She eased her body against his, ensuring that as much of her as possible was touching him.

After a few minutes, they could smell cooking.

'It'll be burnt,' she said.

'I can't think of a better reason for letting it burn.'

They sat at the table and she glanced at him. Now she knew what the phrase *making love* really meant.

I had sex with my husband for years, she thought, but I don't remember passion or tenderness. I don't remember feeling like this.

'Stay,' she said. 'Sleep with me in my bed.'

He was quiet. Then he pulled her to him, kissed

her hair and said, 'Okay, I will.'

In the middle of the night she listened to his breathing.

It's this, she thought, reaching out to touch his skin. It's his presence, next to me, all night. It's the way he drew me into him as we drifted off to sleep, as if I'm being kept safe. It's the little, considerate things he does. I was lying when I said it was a practice falling in love. More nights like this and I will be desperate to hold on to him, then his world will tumble down and I will be responsible.

The image of a pair of scales came into her head, with herself, alone, on one side and his family on the other. He could tip the balance and she knew which way he would go. She moved closer.

'This moment,' she whispered to herself, 'has to be enough.'

The first section of Fell Walkers is set on Loughrigg Fell, which is between Ambleside and Grasmere in the Lake District.

The narrative leading up to this scene and the aftermath have a pivotal place in the novel, **Walking Apart**.

Fell Walkers was a runner up in the ICB short story award 2015.

Morecambe Bay

The tides are long and low, brown salt water creeping, no waves that suck and blow here, no crashing on the beach in self-proclaiming roar. This corner of the ocean moves quietly, stealthily, filling the briny rivulets, smothering seagrass, drowning sandbanks and footpaths that weave over the marsh. If I look away for a minute to stir a pot, the landscape has changed, the sea swelling below the farm wall in a sheet of water rippling under the hand of the wind.

Each day a man appears, head down, bouncing dog at his heels. He walks with the tides, in a natural rhythm, crossing the reeds and grassy tufts, picking a way through the pools and inlets. When he reaches the strand I continue to watch, old field glasses bringing him closer. If the sun shines, it raises silver on the wet sand and he appears to walk on water, gulls wheeling above him in a scatter of grey.

The footpath skirts our house. Faces glance up and smile, some wave. Usually, they are couples, often with children, but he walks alone, rarely pausing in his stride. I imagine his feet leaving deep footprints, water-filled, then erased on the wide spread of soft sand between the salt grasses and the sea.

For a week, he has walked without his dog. This evening, his figure seems transparent, shimmering in the late sunshine. He stumbles, throws a brief look, his eyes meeting mine before he recovers and tilts his hat against the wind. The glance has chilled my soul, sent me reeling with the chasm of his grief, hollow and desperate. I leave my chores and stand by the window as he heads out into the bay.

Rain spatters the pane, blurs the image. I open the casement and follow his progress. When walkers reach firm sand, they turn left or right, but he pursues a westward line, a dark, diminishing smudge. I dare not blink for fear of losing him.

Jake returns from work, closes the window, berates me for tasks left undone and the spray on my clothes. I return his kiss, brew tea. I look out to sea, where weak sunlight polishes the sands. The lonely figure still walks.

Jake throws a newspaper on the table.

'A body washed up,' he says.

'Local?'

He shrugs and turns away. I am slow with my letters. I ask him to read the article, but he rubs his eyes, claims weariness.

'Lost his dog in The Bay. Neighbour says he'd been missing a few days.'

He turns on the radio, settles into the chair, eyes closed.

I reach for the newspaper. The image of the drowned man is grainy, indistinct.

Out there a speck, still walking.

I bring the page closer to my face, glance up.

Less than a speck.

My hand touches perspiration on my brow, heat flushes my body yet I am shivering.

I scan the horizon.

Gone.

Morecambe bay is a unique place, a kaleidoscope of water and light; sea and sky. The Bay is well known for its treacherous sands and the all too frequent tragedy of those caught by a fast-moving incoming tide.

Moving Pictures

The camera was a simple piece of kit, pocket-sized, taken apart and loaded with film under a tartan picnic rug. Dad was ahead of his time. Everyone else had slides, we had cine. He was a good cameraman, and in the pre-digital age, you picked your moments carefully – there was only one chance to get it right.

After a holiday, we awaited the yellow packets of cine reel to drop through the letterbox, our memories captured in hundreds of tiny images. We clamoured to watch them.

'When they've all come back,' he'd say, 'not before.'

We knew better than to pester but couldn't understand the waiting. When each reel had been accounted for, he spliced them together and we sat in the lounge, children on the floor, adults on chairs. The screen was pulled out, curtains drawn, projector plugged in, and three generations assembled expectantly to watch a re-run of the holiday – our own show.

I'll put the lights out.

No, I will.

We're not ready yet.

Sit down, stop making shadows.

It was a rabbit – couldn't you tell?

A dry smell, dust on the hot bulb, a rapid tick-tick-tick as the narrow length of film caught the spool. Spots flickered and figures capered about in glorious colour.

'Is it real?' my sister asked. 'We're all flat. Perhaps it's people pretending to be us.'

'Moving pictures,' Grampa would say. 'We thought they were just for film stars.'

In a final scene, *The End,* written in the sand, disappeared as the incoming tide washed over the letters. We squealed with delight.

Again, run it again.

Please Dad. I want to see the pitch and put, count my score.

Early memories are mere fragments; the birth of my sisters, walking into school on the first day, finding sixpence and spending it on three sherbet dips. As I grew, my awareness of the world expanded, television and radio brought events into our home and I began to pin my life to songs in the charts, sporting victories, news stories.

1969 was the year I remembered everything; Concorde's first test flight, four acts winning first place in the Eurovision Song Contest, Robin Knox-Johnston sailing solo around the world. I worried over how Dorothy from *The Wizard of Oz* could die of an overdose, why Prince Charles was invested as Prince of Wales and not Prince of England and what made two long-haired celebrities stay in bed for days on end as a protest for peace.

We holidayed in Lytham St Annes. It was only an hour from our Lancashire home, but Grampa said it was far enough. Seven of us crammed into a Hillman Minx, suitcases, a windbreak and deck chairs on the roof, bags around our feet. There were no laws about seat belts; my sisters sat on knees, I perched in the middle.

'Is there a TV?' I heard Dad ask. 'I'm not going if there isn't a TV.'

Mum said she had checked, and yes, there was a television in our flat. Today it would be called an apartment; deluxe, family, bijou. In those days, it was a holiday flat, which usually meant Formica worktops, a gas stove, candlewick bedspreads in lilac or lemon and your own key.

I wasn't bothered about a telly – we'd never had one on holiday before. We wouldn't be rushing back from the beach to watch the scant hour of children's programmes, starting with *Jackanory*, finishing with *The Magic Roundabout.* And in any case, the *Blue Peter* presenters would be off on their summer holiday to Kenya or Scotland or somewhere else I had never been.

When we arrived, the landlady, a strong-faced woman, introduced herself as Mrs Watt. She showed us to our rooms.

Grampa and I joked about her name.

What's your name?

Watt.

You shouldn't say what, you should say pardon.

Mrs Watt?

Mrs Who?'

No, not Who, Watt!

We thought it was funny. I repeated the joke to my sisters and we rolled around laughing on the beds.

Mrs Watt had a boxer dog that lived in the yard. We had to walk past him on our way back from the beach.

'He's called Jason,' she said. 'He won't touch you, love.'

Dog owners always say that. I never believe them. I was scared of dogs, and this one barked.

'Jason the basin,' Grampa sang.

'It won't bite,' I murmured.

'Of course not. He's just saying hello.'

I hated that dog, refused to walk past the slavering, beastly thing on my own.

Every day was the beach. It never rained. Dad put up the striped windshield, got out the deck chairs and we'd settle in for the day.

Dad, dig us a hole.

A deep hole, bigger than anyone else's hole, because we had metal spades, not plastic, and Dad would scoop away the soft, slippery sand with his big hands to uncover the damp, stick-together stuff beneath. The hole would deepen, a pile of sand grow, then he'd throw us all in.

Dad, build us a helter-skelter.

A helter-skelter – hours of fun – a sand castle as big as me, with a channel around its walls for a tennis ball to wind a way to the bottom. We got clever. We dug down so the ball went over a bridge, under a tunnel and dropped in the hole. We needed cine coverage of that feat of engineering.

Dad, make us a motorboat.

A motor boat, shaped in sand, two seats in the front, two in the back and we would ride the high seas to faraway lands and places of adventure.

'Dad needs a rest now,' Mum would say.

At lunchtime, Nana brought egg sandwiches and we munched them on the beach, grit on your fingers, in your mouth, crunching between your teeth.

When the slinky tide came in, gathering speed across the long, low beach, it was a moment to paddle and swim and splash in the little waves. We made the most of it as the water sidled away all too soon, disappearing in the distance, leaving hard ripples in the sand that hurt the underside of little feet. Grampa, in shirt and tie with trouser legs rolled up, walked out with me. We followed the ocean's retreat and I collected shells in a bucket.

Before bed, Mum plastered our arms and legs with calamine lotion to soothe our sunburnt skin. We slipped between the nylon sheets covered in chalky pinkness and slept the deep-lidded sleep of children overdosed on fresh air.

Grampa was our best friend. He had endless patience. One morning he took us to the model boating pool. We were in home-sewn matching dresses, with T-bar sandals and white ankle socks. People stared at us, smiled, pointed us out as sisters. I liked the attention, but it was becoming a little embarrassing. Pity my youngest sister who seemed to wear the same dress for years as clothes were handed down.

We leant against the low wall around the pool. I recall a fresh morning, early sunshine on the water, reaching out with a hooked stick to pull in the little boat that Dad had made during the previous winter evenings. It had batteries and a motor and went like a dream across the pool. I sent it to my sister who turned it back to me, then we set the rudder so it described a perfect circle over and over again. We carried it back to the flat, proud of having the best boat, desperate to tell how we had been the envy of other children.

But Nana wouldn't listen when we walked in. She looked at us in horror, pointed to our dresses, streaked across the front where we had leant over the wall.

'Look at them, Arthur,' she protested. 'They were clean on this morning.'

We were sponged down but we weren't blamed and I took off the dress and changed into shorts and t-shirt.

'Where's Dad? I want to tell him about the boat.'

'He's in the lounge.'

Dad was watching the news.

'Have they got there yet?' I asked.

'No,' he said. 'But they've launched the rocket. Won't be long, now.'

I don't remember who gave us spending money, but we always had some to buy a toy or feed the arcade machines on the pier, or buy sweets. That year, I spent my pocket money on books. I had moved on from Enid Blyton's *Faraway Tree* and discovered *The Famous Five.*

We were enjoying a lovely holiday in Lytham St Annes, I didn't need to escape, but climbing into those stories was magical. They took me to Kirrin Island, swimming in the sea, rowing the boat through treacherous rocks, making camp beneath the ruined castle. I was George or Anne, (never one of the boys) down the well, in the dungeons looking for ingots. Then the second book and the third, with the nasty Stick family, the fourth in the secret passages at Smuggler's Top. Before the end of the fortnight I'd travelled the country lanes in a gypsy caravan and finally, in book six, returned to Kirrin Island, where Uncle Quentin was in great danger and needed rescuing by the kids. Ask me about the plot, the characters – I can still tell you fifty years later. Dad took some cine of me reading on the beach, my little sister doing gymnastics, trying to attract my attention.

I hardly look up.

I'd never heard of ginger beer, but I remember asking for it. Orange squash or tea were the usual offerings and I don't recall the adults having a tipple. Our meals were simple. We never ate out, perhaps got fish and chips once in a while, but it would have been ham salads or fish fingers and new potatoes. Nana might make a jelly and open a tin of mandarin segments, Carnation milk poured over the top. We didn't know what pasta was, hardly ever had rice and thought curry was for foreigners. Dad and Grampa weren't big eaters, so it was tea, as we say in Lancashire, then a couple of hours walk along the prom ending at the pier.

There's nothing quite like a thick-bodied snake of old pennies in your hand, heavy with metallic promise turning clean hands grubby. Penny Falls, Cliff Hanger – the machines enticed us with their lights and monotonous tunes.

Look at this one, they're hanging off the edge!

Wait, not yet.

Now – no you've missed it.

NOW!

Angle the chute, pick exactly the right moment when the slider is back, then the coin falls flat and you watch as it pushes the others closer to the cliff edge. Feed in a few more then jump up and down as they fall to the silver tray with a heavy clatter.

'I'm still up,' Grampa used to say when our hoard was usually spent. I'm sure he kept a few extra in his pocket.

We walked to the end of the pier, put our faces to the weather-beaten wooden boards to see the beach below. The wind tangled our hair and we tasted salt on our lips.

Dad put the television on when we got back.

'They've landed,' he announced.

I bounced into an armchair. 'Let's watch them get out?'

Dad laughed. 'They're not getting out just yet.'

'Why?'

'They have to rest.'

Rest? They've landed on the moon. *The Famous Five* didn't rest when they pulled the dinghy up the beach on Kirrin Island. They unpacked, set off to explore, made camp in a cave, ate a huge picnic. Then they might think about a rest.

'Go to bed,' Dad said. 'It'll be the middle of the night before they do anything. I'll wake you up.'

Sunlight filtered through the thin curtains. I watched a spider on the lampshade for a moment and realised no-one had woken me. I dressed with slow, careful movements so as not to disturb my sisters and went in to the lounge where Dad lay dozing on the sofa.

And there it was, a grainy image on the small screen of a spaceman bouncing about on the grey surface. I went closer to the set.

'Is it real?' I whispered. 'It's like a *Blue Peter* model.'

Dad opened his eyes. 'Of course it's real. It's on TV isn't it?'

We sat for a while and watched. Grampa came in, newspaper under his arm. He took off his flat cap and stared at the screen.

'Moving pictures,' he remarked, 'from the moon. Whatever next?'

'Venus,' I suggested, 'the Milky Way?'

'Impossible,' Dad said. 'Too far.'

'Your Nana and I thought Venice was too far,' Grampa said. 'Then we were on an aeroplane to Italy.'

I looked at the television, at Armstrong and Aldrin in spacesuits, at the Lunar Module, flimsy and delicate, seemingly made out of silver paper and sticky-back plastic.

We were accepting the impossible, witnessing the incredible, desperately believing something we couldn't quite understand.

I put a hand in the pocket of my shorts and touched yesterday's shell collection as the world expanded into a vastness of hope and optimism and possibility.

The 1960s proved to be a decade of rapid change. The end of the war was still a recent memory, but to post war children, it seemed like a period consigned to the history books.

We had toys, but the absence of technology and social media gave us a freedom to create our own games and adventures.

Few ventured abroad and for years, we holidayed on the nearby Fylde coast. We loved every day. Our activities were simple and with the family together (we were sometimes joined by both sets of grandparents) we needed nothing more.

The decade began with uncertainty, although I was too young to remember this, and ended with one of mankind's greatest achievements.

We still have, and still watch, the cine film.

About the Author

When she left the school in Lancashire where she was headteacher for eleven years, Catherine Finch moved to France with her husband. With time on her hands, she settled down to write a novel.

Walking Apart was published in January 2018. It follows a couple in their mid-fifties through a difficult year when retirement seems to offer as many problems as it does opportunities. The Ribble Valley in Lancashire, the Lake District and Melbourne, Australia provide the backdrop to a story of love, complex relationships and control.

Holding On Letting Go is Catherine's second novel. The French countryside, with its rugged hills, wide rivers and characterful villages, provides a colourful setting and will surely entice readers to explore this area further.

Walking Alone, a sequel to Walking Apart, takes the reader along the beautiful and challenging Camino de Santiago pilgrimage in Northern Spain.

Alongside her writing, the author also enjoys walking and believes that the two activities go hand in hand. Putting one foot in front of the other gives her the space to review ideas, listen to her characters and plan future narratives.

Novels are available in electronic format and in paperback. They can be ordered through the author's website, where information about the bookshops who support her work, and the latest news about her writing can be found.

Discover more about Catherine and her writing at:
chaffinchbooks.co.uk

Walking Apart

The first book in the series about David and Helen Richards and their family.

A must read for those who like to meet new characters and get a deep insight into their lives and relationships, this book is for anyone who likes walking, works in education or has ever been in love!

This book is beautifully and sensitively written. It covers the relationship dynamics between a long-married couple coping with change as later life presents its challenges. Page after page flows as you are taken into the world within the book. I read it over one day and will read it again. I sincerely hope there will be further books from this author. A truly memorable first book

This is a sensitively rendered story of a relationship at a crossroads, and deals with subjects such as love, retirement, marriage, and ageing in an entertaining way. Especially good in observing and pinpointing significance in the details of the rituals of everyday life. Absorbing.

Easy to read and hard to put down. I enjoyed every page and the journey each chapter revealed. The writer's exploration of ordinary people's feelings and life decisions made a realistic and interesting read.

I was gripped from beginning to end. Loved the Lancashire setting.

Walking Alone

The story of David and Helen continues.

The novel has depth beyond just being an interesting, well-told story; it challenges the reader to bring their own opinions to the experience.

I've really enjoyed reading Walking Alone and it has inspired me to walk the Camino. I couldn't sleep until I'd finished it - unputdownable!

This is an excellent read with believable, down-to-earth characters, real problems and superb settings, particularly fascinating as it takes the reader along the Camino de Santiago pilgrimage. Catherine paints a vivid picture of what the various towns and villages are like - the sights, sounds and smells.
I highly recommend this book.

A particularly strong point of Catherine Finch (and something that many authors neglect) is her ability to 'set the scene'. In Walking Alone, the reader is taken to the plains, mountains and cities of northern Spain to tread the paths thousands have paced before.

This is a vast landscape, where the weather and the terrain can swallow the pilgrim physically and mentally, spitting out the remains, which will never be the same again. A fabulous read. A fitting sequel to Walking Apart. I, for one, hope that this story is not yet over.

Holding On Letting Go

A sumptuous setting in rural France

I loved this book and couldn't put it down. An unexpected and distressing event kept the narrative alive until the very end. Vivid descriptions of French life give this novel a sumptuous background. I am determined to visit this area of France to walk in the footsteps of the characters.

Brilliant! I had a couple of very enjoyable days (and nights) reading the book. I loved it. It's a great plot and I enjoyed getting to know the characters.

A great read. I know the places the characters visit, so I also know how brilliantly they are portrayed and described. But even the little details are just right. This is a real-life story – it's hot, it's dry, running a business and having gites is NOT a romantic holiday; it's a brutal way to make a living and there is isolation in a rural area in France, away from family and the culture of your childhood.

A novel that completely absorbed my attention over two days. I was warmed by the essence of family life, the relationships between some of the characters, the sunshine. I could taste the wine, smell the dry grass, visualise the gorgeous scenery. Yet this is also a book which raises issues and left me pondering long after I had put it down. Highly recommended.

Acknowledgements

I would like to thank;

Anita, for leading the Parisot Writing Group with such inspiration and enthusiasm,

members of the group, both past and present, for their critical feedback and support,

Sheila, for editing the final draft, which is a task far greater than merely spotting typos,

and Gary, who read and listened to the stories, even though he usually prefers crime thrillers.

Catherine Finch
January 2021

catherinesfinch7@gmail.com
www.chaffinchbooks.co.uk
Twitter: @chatffinch
Instagram: catherinesfinch

Name	Country/region	Date

Printed in Great Britain
by Amazon

54686597R00073